Love on the Nile

by

Ellie Gray

Love on the Nile

Contact Information: info@thewildrosepress.com

Cover Art by *Diana Carlile*

The Wild Rose Press, Inc.
PO Box 708
Adams Basin, NY 14410-0708
Visit us at www.thewildrosepress.com

Publishing History
First Edition, 2022
Trade Paperback ISBN 978-1-5092-3988-7
Digital ISBN 978-1-5092-3989-4

Previously Published Tirgearr Publishing, 2016
Published in the United States of America

"You are beautiful," he said softly, gently lifting her chin with his finger and gazing into her eyes, emphasized this evening by a soft line of kohl. "Nice eye make-up."

Again, that hint of colour spreading across her delicate cheekbones. "I found a picture of Nefertiti and tried to copy the eyeliner." She shrugged. "Do you think I look all right? It's not too much?"

"Stunning. You take my breath away."

He was rewarded with a smile and a brief kiss that was over far too quickly when she stepped back to regard him critically. He turned full circle, arms outstretched before raising a quizzical eyebrow. "So, what do you think?"

His hair was slicked back from his forehead, and the false moustache hopefully looked realistic. The old-fashioned tweed suit, with the rather baggy trousers, didn't look as bad as he had expected and were actually very comfortable. But he was unable to read anything from her expression as she stood with her head on one side, her critical gaze taking in his appearance from head to toe. His body tingled in response to her light gaze, and his breath quickened at the unexpected sensuality of the moment.

"Howard Carter, I presume," she said at last, a smile curving her lips. "Though I didn't realise Mr. Carter was so very handsome."

Praise for Ellie Gray

"Ellie Gray has written a tender but sassy romance set in the beautiful surroundings of Egypt. Her setting descriptions are so vivid that readers will feel the sand under their feet!"

~ InD'Tale Magazine.

"The author paints a wonderful picture of Egypt, a place I have always wanted to visit. I could 'see' the characters in this book, they are described so well."

~Pollyanna

"Love on the Nile is engaging, romantic and left me with a smile!"

~Rae Reads

Dedication

For Joseph and Abigail - you are my world

Chapter One

The hotel's cool interior provided a blessed relief from the stifling heat and bustling streets of mid-afternoon Cairo as Natasha Morgan followed the porter along the bright airy corridor. Their footsteps made no sound on the royal blue, thick pile carpet, and when Natasha glanced back, she could see her brother, Nicky, reading and whispering the name of each suite they passed. She gave a weary smile, looking forward to sinking into a comfortable armchair in the hope it would ease her aching back. It had been a long day.

This trip was something she had wanted to do for years, and now she was finally fulfilling her childhood dream; a trip to the ancient land of the pharaohs. Determined to have an adventure rather than their usual ready-made package holiday, she had made no plans other than to book flights to Cairo for herself and Nicky, and to accept an invitation to stay — at least initially — with her aunt in the suite of rooms she traditionally rented over the summer.

Not that she hadn't done her homework. Although it was a world away from her little terraced house in the heart of Yorkshire, she felt as if she had been researching this holiday for most of her life, and had made a careful list of the temples and ancient sites she wanted to visit. She had deliberately not pre-booked any excursions or sightseeing tours, wanting to allow herself time to get a feel for the place before making any set plans. But now that she was finally here, the thought of such a loose itinerary left her with butterflies in her stomach, and nervous tension pulling across her shoulders. A run-of-the-mill package holiday beside a beach suddenly looked quite appealing.

Lost in thought, she rubbed at the painful knot at the top of her spine, and only narrowly avoided bumping into the porter when he stopped beside an impressive set of polished, dark wooden doors. A quick glance at the name plate reassured Natasha that they had arrived at the Cleopatra Suite, and she smiled, tipping the young man what she hoped was enough, before turning to her brother.

"Well, Nicky, we're here at last. We made it."

He gave a bright smile and nodded his head enthusiastically. "Thank goodness. I'm starving."

She rolled her eyes, a reluctant smile tugging at her lips as she knocked on the door.

"Why are you knocking? The lady downstairs gave us a card thingy to get in."

Her smile broadened, and she turned to her brother, her head on one side as she looked at him in amusement. At first glance no-one would ever guess that this twenty-six-year-old man had the mental age of a ten-year-old, a result of the developmental delay he had been born with.

"Yes, we have a key-card, but these are still Aunt Lucy's rooms and we're her guests. It's polite to knock first, just to let her know we're here."

Nicky's expression told her that he thought she was being overly sensitive, but his only response was a resigned shrug. They waited patiently for a few seconds, but when there was no response, Natasha swiped her key-card across the electronic lock, and pushed open the door.

"Told you we should have just gone in."

She ignored Nicky's stage whisper, and walked into the narrow entrance hall. Doors led off each side of the hallway before opening out into a large living room, where she saw her aunt sitting by French windows, in animated discussion with a man she did not recognise. Seated with their backs to the door, the two appeared completely unaware of their visitors' arrival.

"I'm an archaeologist, Lucy, not a tour guide. Your relatives may well be pleasant, but I have no desire to shepherd them around Egypt, answering their predictably inane questions about ancient myths and customs, while at the same time complaining about the heat." There was a pause as he caught his breath and gave a tight smile in an obvious effort to soften his words. "However, I can put them in touch with a reputable company, if that would help."

Weary and already a little stressed by her first foray into this exotic country, Natasha felt a stab of irritation at this stranger's dismissive words. She stepped into the room. "Well, I can assure you, you've no need to put yourself out on our account. We neither need nor want your assistance, and I equally have no desire to spend my holiday being...*shepherded*, was that the word you used? Yes, shepherded around Egypt by you."

Both he and her aunt turned in surprise.

"Natasha, darling!" The rather stout woman levered herself from the chair, and swiftly crossed the room to throw her arms around her niece.

Breathing in the familiar perfume, and leaning into her aunt's protective embrace, Natasha's irritation dissipated as quickly as it had appeared, and she closed her eyes against the sudden and unexpected tears of relief at having finally arrived at their destination. "Oh, Aunt Lucy, it's so good to see you." Her voice was muffled against Lucy's shoulder, and she took a deep breath before stepping back and smiling. "It's been so long. I can't believe we're actually here at last."

"It's wonderful to see you, Natasha. I've missed you both so much." Lucy lifted a hand to cup her niece's face before turning to Nicky, hands on her ample hips as she scrutinised him critically.

"Oh, you always were like two peas in a pod. And, I have to say Nicky, you have grown into a very handsome young man. You have no idea how happy I am that you came."

"Hello, Aunty Lucy, how are you?" Nicky briefly returned her embrace before stepping back, securing the baseball cap a little tighter on his head, and asking the question foremost in his mind. "Can I have something to eat?"

Lucy shook her head with a smile and turned to the stranger, who had so far remained silent throughout. "Kyle, this is my nephew Nicky, and my niece Natasha. I'm pleased to see that at least one thing never changes, and that is Nicky's appetite."

She caught Nicky's arm and led him off to the far side of the room. "Come on, I've got some of your favourite biscuits over here in this cupboard."

Kyle's gaze followed her younger brother thoughtfully, his eyes narrowed, and Natasha felt the familiar churning in the pit of her stomach, trying to anticipate at what point he would realise Nicky had learning difficulties. She automatically tried to deflect that scrutiny, moving further into the room, and feeling a sense of relief when Kyle's gaze immediately swung towards her.

"Natasha Morgan," she introduced herself, and held out her hand.

"So I gather." His gaze drew over her face, and she was uncomfortably aware of her earlier, rather waspish response to what was probably quite a reasonable conversation he had been having with her aunt. He pushed himself from the chair to tower over her, his hair shining blue-black in the pale moonlight streaming in through the open window. Tall as she was, Natasha had to tilt her head back to meet his startlingly blue eyes. He was younger than she had initially thought, probably in his mid-thirties — just a few years older than herself.

There was a pause before he replied. "Kyle Richardson."

He took her hand briefly, offering a firm cool handshake, before returning to his chair, long legs stretched out before him and crossed at the ankles.

"I'm sorry you overheard our conversation; I had no idea you were there."

His voice was deep and husky, and his gaze once again followed her movements when she sank into the seat Lucy had recently vacated.

She nodded and spread her hands expressively, shrugging her slim shoulders. "I'm sorry if I sounded… irritated. It's been a really long day, and I wasn't expecting Aunt Lucy to arrange a personal guide for us. Please, it's not a problem, and we don't want… um, we don't need a guide. I'm sure you have better things to do with your time."

His mouth twitched as if in amusement at her

inadvertent slip of the tongue, but whatever he was about to say was lost when Lucy and Nicky returned, the latter clutching a packet of chocolate-covered biscuits.

"Oh, you've introduced yourselves. Excellent." Lucy beamed at them, clapping her hands together. "I'm sure we're all going to have a wonderful time together."

"I was just explaining that Nicky and I are quite happy to find our own way around Egypt," Natasha cut in quickly. "There is no need for Mr. Richardson to trouble himself."

"Nonsense." Her aunt fixed Kyle with a rather piercing gaze. "Don't think I'm letting you wriggle out of this one, Kyle. You owe me a number of favours, and I am now calling one of them in. For heaven's sake, I haven't seen you in close to two years, and I happen to know for a fact that you haven't taken a break for longer than that. It's high time you did."

Natasha observed this outburst with some surprise, having hardly ever heard her aunt speak so sharply. She risked a glance towards Kyle; he was reclined in his chair, arms folded over his chest with a somewhat amused gleam in his blue eyes. He remained silent, obviously expecting Lucy to continue her reprimand.

"You can clean up that boat of yours, get your crew together and… and away we'll all go." Lucy stood there rather breathlessly, holding up her hand when he opened his mouth to respond. "No, it's no use arguing and, yes, you did hear me correctly. I'm coming with you. I couldn't possibly allow Natasha aboard your boat without a chaperone."

Her last remark drew a simultaneous response.

"Now you're being ridiculous." Kyle sat forward immediately.

"Oh, please." Natasha waved a hand at her aunt in disgust.

Lucy's face broke into a grin, and she turned to Nicky, who was standing to one side and munching on his chocolate biscuits, his eyes moving from one to the other.

"They're like children, aren't they? So easy to wind up." She turned back, shaking her head. "I was joking about acting as chaperone, of course, although I am perfectly serious about joining you aboard your boat. I doubt I shall accompany you around many of the temples, but I can think of nothing I would enjoy more than a gentle cruise along the Nile. It's been quite a while since I last did that."

"But, Aunt Lucy, I haven't even worked out what we're going to do yet, and I'm sure Mr. Richardson can't just drop…whatever it is he does…at a moment's notice." Natasha turned to Kyle for help, confident he would agree with her.

His eyes met hers for a long moment, a moment during which she felt an unexpected flutter in the pit of her stomach and an awareness that, for some reason, her heart had begun to beat a little faster. His expression was unreadable, and only when he broke eye contact to push himself out of his chair and turn to the older woman, did Natasha realise she had been holding her breath.

"Lucy, you know why I've been away so long," he said evenly.

"Yes, I do know." Her voice softened, and she moved across the room to lay a gentle hand on his arm. "And you know what my thoughts are on that. Enough is enough."

The air was filled with an expectant silence as Lucy

held his gaze, until he gave a crooked smile and shook his head. "I can count on one hand the number of times I've actually won an argument with you, so I shall back down gracefully. Let me make some calls, and I'll be in touch later tomorrow."

Natasha stared at him in dismay. Why was he agreeing to her aunt's ridiculous suggestion? This was meant to be *her* holiday. Hers and Nicky's. She didn't want to spend it with a stranger.

"But…"

Ignoring her angry gaze, Kyle bent to pick up his hat, nodding briefly in her direction. "Miss Morgan, Nicky."

At this point Nicky's face broke into a grin, and he hastily swallowed his mouthful of biscuit. "Wow, you look like that guy from my favourite movie!"

Unable to completely stifle the gasp of surprised laughter, Natasha hurriedly turned it into a cough when Kyle glanced in her direction. She avoided his gaze as if suddenly finding the painting on the near wall very interesting, while Nicky excitedly talked about the famous adventurer archaeologist from the films he loved so much. She had to admit, now that Nicky had mentioned it, there was a certain resemblance, although it was more in his style of clothing than any physical similarity. Tall and lean, he had the air of a man comfortable in his skin and confident in his ability to handle himself. Despite her reluctance to spend her holiday in the company of this man, she couldn't ignore the fact that he was the archetypal tall, dark, and handsome hero.

"Do you have a whip and a gun too, like he does?" Nicky continued, his green eyes wide with the wonderment you would expect to find in a ten-year-old, not a young man in his mid-twenties. "Cos, that would be really cool."

Acutely aware of Kyle's narrowed gaze, Natasha found herself holding her breath, recognising the sudden awareness within his glance. She steeled herself for a negative reaction, for him to ignore or dismiss her brother; or perhaps he would just pity him. None of those reactions would be surprising or unusual, but even though she knew Nicky wouldn't understand or be upset by them, every time she encountered them, it broke her heart.

"Well, I'm afraid I don't have a whip or a gun like he does," Kyle admitted after a brief pause. Then he leaned closer to the younger man and whispered conspiratorially, but loudly, "But if I did, I wouldn't bring it with me when I have tea with your aunt. I'd be worried she might just get mad and shoot me."

Nicky gave a hoot of delighted laughter, and clenched his fists together in excitement, turning to his sister. "Tash, this is going to be sooo good. We're not going on holiday, we're going on an adventure!"

She couldn't help but glance across to see Kyle's reaction, and was surprised and relieved to see his face creased with a genuine smile. "Well, I can't guarantee we'll be running from huge rolling boulders, and I certainly wouldn't like to get trapped in a pyramid, but I'm sure we can find something interesting to do."

He lifted a hand to squeeze Nicky's shoulder, planted a kiss on Lucy's cheek, and nodded briefly in Natasha's direction before leaving the room.

"He's brill, Tash, isn't he? Don't you think he's ace?"

"Yes, Nicky. He's um…he's ace." She managed a smile, and tried to ignore the sinking feeling in her stomach, recognising the hero-worship shining from his eyes.

****

Kyle paused in the narrow entrance hall with his hand on the door handle, wondering at this turn of events. When Lucy had called to invite him for afternoon tea after learning that he was back in Cairo, he had not expected to leave that meeting having agreed to spend almost a fortnight hosting two strangers on his boat. He had spent the last few years carefully avoiding those he was close to, Lucy included, and he wondered how he had now managed to allow himself to be manoeuvred into spending time with them. He closed his eyes briefly and shook his head, laughing at his edginess; a fortnight was no time at all, he had nothing to worry about.

He glanced back towards the living room, and smiled slightly at the sight of Nicky hopping from one foot to the other in excitement. Lucy had talked in passing about her niece and nephew numerous times over the years, but had omitted to mention that Nicky obviously had some form of developmental delay. He was an engaging young man, but his sister was another kettle of fish altogether. Her clear green eyes and porcelain skin, framed by glossy, dark hair, ensured that any red-blooded male would give her more than a passing glance. But on first impressions, she was a prickly character with a sharp temper.

As he lingered unobserved in the entrance hall, Kyle watched Nicky and Lucy step out onto the balcony, leaving Natasha alone in the living room. He was surprised to see her bright smile fade and her face take on an altogether more vulnerable expression; her eyes dropping to the floor as she chewed pensively on her lip. He hesitated, aware he should leave, but reluctant to open the door in case the movement caught her attention. His dilemma was solved when Lucy's voice called to her from the balcony, and he saw her chin lift, pasting the bright smile back on her face, before joining them.

He stared into the space where she had been standing just a few seconds before. There was more to this girl than met the eye. No sooner had the thought entered his head, then he caught himself in surprise, and shrugged his shoulders irritably; what did it matter? He had no interest in finding out if his first impression was correct or not. In fact, he had no desire to know anything about her at all.

Chapter Two

Over the next three days, Natasha and Nicky spent their time exploring Cairo, with its fascinating blend of modern and ancient. Natasha enjoyed wandering through the bazaars, quickly becoming confident in the art of haggling, and learning to ignore the continual pleas for '*baksheesh*'. Despite her initial apprehension, the teeming streets of the old city felt safe, if a little chaotic. She loved the narrow, winding streets where she had to keep her wits about her to avoid being hit by cars and bikes, and even the occasional horse or goat. But her absolute favourite place was the ancient bazaar at Khan el-Khalili, a maze of canvas-covered streets and courtyards, where every available space from floor to ceiling was crammed full of spices, rugs, gold, silver, and copper. She could hardly believe her eyes at the amount of merchandise on sale; it was like walking into a scene from one of the old Saturday afternoon matinees, where the hero or heroine finally find the fabled hidden treasure of some long-lost king or, in this case, pharaoh.

However, more often than not, she found herself sitting on a step drinking tea with one of the friendly shopkeepers, all of whom spoke excellent English, while Nicky, a talented artist and rarely to be seen without his pad and pencil, captured the scene in his sketchbook.

Lucy occasionally accompanied them around the chaotic streets, but more usually it was just the two of them, as it had been for the last twelve years. With a slight pang of guilt, Natasha couldn't help but feel relieved when she neither heard from nor saw Kyle Richardson during those few days. Her brother's immediate enthusiasm for the man made her uneasy, and the thought of spending the majority of her holiday in his company bothered her more than she cared to admit. She had worked hard to be able to afford this trip to Egypt for herself and Nicky, had looked forward to seeing her aunt, and was now more than a little unsettled that it seemed she had to share it with a complete stranger.

****

The day before they were due to board Kyle's boat, Natasha and Nicky visited the Egyptian Museum of Antiquities, where they spent almost the entire day browsing the displays housing ancient artefacts and treasures. Nicky was in his element, and she knew there was no point trying to persuade her brother to simply buy a brochure instead of drawing his favourite pieces, so she contented herself in perusing the museum without him, battling with the other tourists who crowded the rooms.

She spent most of her time in the Amarna room where artefacts from the reign of Akhenaten and Nefertiti were housed. From an early age, she had developed a keen interest — some might say an obsession — with Ancient Egypt and, as a teenager, was hardly to be seen without a book on the subject. Her particular interest more recently was in the Amarna period, and here in the museum she was able to gaze upon the elongated features of Akhenaten's statue. Having only ever seen photographs, she found it breathtaking in real life. She knew some viewed the odd facial features as strange and bizarre, but Natasha had always seen a strange form of beauty in the gentle smile and eyes of the long-dead pharaoh.

Slowly making her way around the rooms, she marvelled at the segment of painted pavement which had been carefully removed from the ancient site at Tel-el-Amarna, and the colourful frescoes depicting exotic plants and geese. She gazed in awe, imagining the chatter of ancient men and women as they walked over this very pavement thousands of years before. Despite the hordes of visitors crowding the museum, being able to see the beautifully carved artefacts that she had only previously seen in photographs fulfilled all Natasha's expectations, and she found herself relaxing. This was what she had come to Egypt for. This was her holiday, and she was determined to enjoy it, even if that did mean sharing it with a stranger.

****

Early next morning Lucy, Natasha, and Nicky arrived by taxi to begin their cruise along the Nile in Kyle's boat. Expecting a sleek, modern cruiser, Natasha stared open-mouthed at the beautiful boat moored alongside the quay.

Bobbing gently in the water, painted bright white with polished wooden trim and towering sails at either end of the deck, this beautifully preserved boat gleamed like new. It was a dahabeeyah; a vessel more commonly seen cruising along the Nile during the late 1800s. She had read about these boats, and seen photographs and drawings, but never expected to actually sail in one. Written in black script along the bow were the words *Aten's Dream*.

Her eyes swept from the wooden steps leading from the main deck up to the canopied sun deck above, where she could imagine relaxing in the shade while the world drifted by. It would feel like stepping back in time.

"Catching flies, Miss Morgan?"

Kyle strode past her to board the boat, and she closed her mouth with a snap, colouring slightly when she realised that she had indeed been standing open-mouthed, while Lucy and Nicky had already boarded with their luggage. She picked up her suitcases and hurried aboard, muttering darkly to herself.

Not quite sure where Kyle had gone, she stepped through the nearest door, and found herself in a narrow corridor with doors on either side. She hesitated, blinking in the semi-darkness after the bright sunlight, but then saw him opening one of the doors towards the bottom of the short corridor.

"Yours," he flung over his shoulder, before disappearing through another door at the end and closing it behind him.

She stared after him for a few seconds before poking her tongue out at the closed door. The man already had an infuriating knack for irritating her, and had obviously got out of bed on the wrong side this morning. As she slowly made her way down the corridor to what would seem to be her cabin, she heard doors banging and drawers being opened and closed, and assumed that Nicky and Lucy were already unpacking in their rooms.

Quietly closing her cabin door, Natasha sank onto the king-sized bed and looked around her, trying without success to find something to dislike about the room. It was quite spacious, certainly more than big enough for her, spotlessly clean, and comfortably furnished with an en-suite bathroom. It even had a small sofa beside the window, where she could imagine sitting and relaxing as she watched the world go by. The internal décor continued the external theme of pristine white walls with polished wooden floors and fittings.

Flopping back on the bed, she looked up at the ceiling to find the light fitting had a fan attached to keep the room cool. Dammit! It was perfect; she couldn't have wished for better accommodation. Despite the fact that the boat belonged to Kyle Richardson, she adored it.

At the soft tapping on her door, she sprang to her feet, fully expecting it to be Kyle with more sarcastic comments. Relief flooded through her when she saw Lucy standing in the doorway, a rather worried expression on her face.

"Hello, Natasha dear," she smiled. "I was going to ask if you wanted to join me up on deck for a cool drink, but if you're too tired…"

"No, no, I'm fine. I was just… you know, checking if the bed was okay."

Deciding she could unpack later, she followed her aunt to the sun deck where someone had thoughtfully placed a carafe of iced lemonade on one of the tables beneath the shady canopy.

"Nicky and Kyle seem to be getting on famously." Lucy sounded pleased.

Sitting in one of the rattan chairs, and closing her eyes to lean back in the shady warmth, Natasha remained silent, her lips tightening as she bit back a comment.

"Oh, Tash dear, I know you and Kyle have started off on the wrong foot, and I agree he can be a shade difficult at times, but really, he is one of my dearest friends." Lucy gave a sigh. "Your uncle thought of Kyle as the son he never had."

Natasha reluctantly opened her eyes to see the worry

clouding her aunt's face, and she forced a smile to her lips. "Well, I probably got us off to a bad start by snapping at him when we first met, so perhaps that's why he seems so irritable with me. I'm sure we'll get on okay. If Uncle Joe liked him then he can't be all that bad, can he?"

Lucy breathed an obvious sigh of relief, and settled back in her chair while Natasha poured them both a glass of lemonade.

"It's been so much harder this winter, Tash," said Lucy quietly, swirling her glass slightly as the melting ice-cubes tinkled. "I know it sounds silly, but this last month or so I've felt as if Joe is still... well, I've caught faint traces of his tobacco smoke, and quite a few times I could have sworn he was in the next room. I've even called his name and gone to check, but of course, he wasn't there."

She reached into the neck of her short-sleeved blouse, to where she always kept a tissue tucked into the straps of her underwear, and blew her nose loudly.

Natasha blinked away sudden tears of sadness, both for her aunt's distress and her own grief at her uncle's death two years ago.

"You're bound to have good days and bad days still, Aunt Lucy," she soothed. "It hasn't been that long, and being here in Egypt is always going to bring back memories; you and Uncle Joe spent so much time here."

"I've hardly left Egypt since his death, but lately it's been more difficult." Lucy shook her head before blowing her nose one final time. "I'm just being a silly old woman."

"I don't think anyone could ever call you that," smiled Natasha, favouring her aunt with a wry glance as she leant forward to reach for her glass.

"Nevertheless, it's why I've been so selfish, and forced both Kyle and myself on you," Lucy carried on seriously. "I know this isn't what you planned, but I couldn't bear to spend the next month on my own in that suite of rooms. When Kyle arrived back in Cairo just as you were due to arrive, it seemed as if it would solve all our problems."

She paused for a moment before offering a rather watery smile. "Well, when I say 'our problems', of course I meant my own. Anyway, I thought if I could persuade Kyle to take us on his boat, then you could see all your sites without the worry of transport, Kyle would get the break he never gives himself, and I…well, I would get to spend all my time with the three people who are most dear to me in this world."

Natasha gazed thoughtfully at her aunt, noticing for the first time how tired she looked. Lucy had always been a vital, outgoing woman, not one to suffer fools gladly, but underneath her bossy manner, she was a kind and caring soul. Sharing her Egyptologist husband's passion for Egypt, she had spent most of her married life there, returning to England only for brief periods to visit Natasha and Nicky as their only living relative. When Joe died two years ago, she initially returned to England but had been too homesick to stay away for any length of time, and had since returned to spend more time in Egypt than in her native country.

Now Natasha wondered if her aunt was not coping without her husband as well as she had first appeared. Although still a rather stout woman, Lucy had lost weight, and there were more strands of grey in her sandy hair. If Lucy was being selfish, then perhaps Natasha was equally so, wishing that she and Nicky could spend their holiday alone.

Reflecting on the situation, she had to admit that her aunt's arrangements were far better than anything she could have arranged herself; the only real fly in the ointment was having to spend time with Kyle Richardson. She bit her lip, perhaps she ought to give him the benefit of the doubt. After all, she could hardly blame the man for being irritated at having to act as a tour guide to two complete strangers for a fortnight, when he had just arrived in Cairo. It was unfair to make a judgement based on the minimal conversations they had shared so far.

But still, she couldn't shake a sense of uneasiness. It wasn't just that he'd been short with her, certainly she'd been rather waspish with him too! No, what worried her was the hero-worship shining from Nicky's eyes whenever Kyle's name was mentioned. A little voice in the back of her head whispered that perhaps she too might fall under his spell, and she blinked in surprise. She shrugged her shoulders, as if to physically shrug away such a ridiculous thought and, with some effort, picked up the threads of their conversation.

"You're not being selfish." She leaned across to hold Lucy's hand. "I'll admit that I was a little apprehensive about having to arrange transport and everything myself. And look at this boat – it's so beautiful. It's like something I've only ever dreamed of."

A sudden clattering of footsteps heralded Nicky's arrival, and he paused at the top of the stairs, red-faced and grinning broadly.

"Hi, Aunt Lucy, hi, Tash." He looked at them, clenching and unclenching his fists with obvious excitement. "This is so cool. Kyle's been showing me how to drive the boat and he says I can help him. That is all right, isn't it, Tash?"

His grin faded a little as if worried Natasha might not approve, but before she could open her mouth, Lucy spoke up.

"Of course it is, Nicky," she patted the chair next to her. "Come and sit down and tell me all about how to *sail* this boat."

"Well, I'm going to unpack." Natasha stood and walked across the deck, tapping the front of Nicky's baseball cap as she passed him so that it dropped down over his eyes. He pushed it up again with a good-humoured frown.

Lucy called after her. "Tash dear, why don't you give Kyle the list of sites you want to visit so he can plan for the tides, and transport... and... whatever else he needs to plan?"

Natasha raised her hand in acknowledgement before disappearing down the stairs and making her way to the cool sanctuary of her cabin.

****

"Amarna? Why on earth would you want to go to Amarna? It's nothing but a few crumbling walls in a barren wasteland."

Natasha had handwritten the list of sites she planned to visit during their ten-day cruise, and given it to Kyle. With a derisive snort, he held the piece of paper towards her, shaking his head at her obvious lack of knowledge.

"There are no magnificent temples and shrines for you to wander around—"

"I know exactly what is at the Amarna site."

"Then you know that no-one other than an

archaeologist would find anything of interest there."

"That's a rather sweeping assumption. I've always been interested in the Amarna period, and would like to see where Akhenaten built his city." Natasha swatted away a particularly annoying fly buzzing between them. "I'd like to see it."

"Then you'll be disappointed."

"Then that's my problem, isn't it?" She held his gaze defiantly. "Mr. Richardson, can you take us to the Amarna site? Because if you can't, then I'll find someone who can." Natasha strove to keep her voice even, and tacked on a tight smile for good measure.

"If you insist on going, then I will take you, of course," he shrugged. "But don't come running to me when it doesn't live up to your romantic ideals."

She snatched the piece of paper from his proffered hand. "Oh, you've no need to worry on that score. Even if Sobek himself were snapping at my heels, I wouldn't come running to you."

With the satisfying image of the crocodile-headed Egyptian god ripping Kyle limb from limb, she turned on her heel and stalked away from him, her satisfaction somewhat short-lived when she realised she had to walk the entire length of the deck before being able to move out of his line of sight. She imagined his eyes following her progress, perhaps lingering on her rear, and fought the urge to glance over her shoulder to see if her instincts were correct.

****

The salon area of the dahabeeyah was beautifully but comfortably furnished in period style, and Natasha once again attempted to stifle her irritation and dislike for the man sitting opposite her, and who was listening intently to Nicky's excited chatter. Had she made her own travel arrangements, she could never have afforded such luxurious accommodation.

"Kyle, that was absolutely delicious. You must give my compliments to the chef." Lucy dabbed her napkin to her lips, and sat back with a contented sigh.

"Perhaps if Mr. Richardson allowed his staff to dine with us, you could have complimented the chef yourself." Natasha smiled sweetly at her aunt, who favoured her with a reproving glance.

"Mahmoud and Nader are always welcome to dine with us," said Kyle, mildly. "For some reason, they have declined the offer on this occasion…maybe the company doesn't appeal."

At that moment Mahmoud, a tall handsome Egyptian, appeared at the table to begin swiftly clearing away the remains of their meal. For such a tall man he moved with surprising grace, and so silently that he gave the impression of appearing out of nowhere. It was difficult to place an age on him, but Natasha guessed he was probably around the same age as Kyle, in his mid-thirties.

Mindful of Kyle's sarcastic comments, she looked up to meet the Egyptian's eye, but he appeared to avoid her glance, and she dropped her own gaze in consternation. Had she somehow offended them, although she couldn't think how? Or perhaps Nicky? She bit her lip. He had spent a good deal of time below deck with Kyle and his crew. What if he had been annoying them?

Staring into her steaming coffee, trying to think of a good reason why Kyle's staff might wish to avoid her, she gave a start when Lucy's voice interrupted her reverie.

"So, tell me, how is Paul?"

"Paul?" She frowned in surprise. "Um, I don't really know, but I assume he's fine. We, er…we aren't together anymore. I haven't seen him for months."

"Oh, Natasha, that's such a shame." Lucy seemed genuinely sorry. "He was such a lovely young man. Do you mind me asking what happened?"

Natasha glanced across the table, and was relieved to see Kyle and Nicky were engrossed in a card game, although Nicky continued to talk without pausing for breath.

"Nothing 'happened', there was no big break-up. Paul got a new job working away, and we both decided that we'd come to a natural end. It was a mutual thing."

"Rubbish," said Lucy crisply. "That young man adored you. I can guess exactly what happened. Did he ask you to go with him, in his new job?"

"Well, yes—"

"Of course he did," Lucy nodded. "And you refused. An excellent excuse to end it and continue treading water through life on your own with Nicky, just as you always have done with anyone who shows an interest in you."

"Aunt Lucy, I—" She stared at the older woman, shocked by her outburst.

"No, I have held my tongue long enough," Lucy interrupted, that same tongue having been loosened by the excellent red wine consumed over dinner. "I have watched you sacrifice your hopes and dreams while you fought to give Nicky the stable home life and support he needed."

"My hopes and dreams?" echoed Natasha weakly.

"I have always admired your strength and

determination to fight for Nicky's rights and independence, but enough is enough."

Lucy paused for breath and another large mouthful of wine, while Natasha could only gape at her, stunned into silence by her aunt's surprising outburst.

"Enough is enough," she repeated, staring beadily at Natasha. "Nicky is a grown man with his own flat and a job. You can't keep using him as an excuse for not committing to a relationship. Nobody likes a martyr, Natasha dear."

That was the final straw. At first, it had been faintly amusing, but now it was insulting and painful.

"I have never, and will never, use Nicky as an excuse for anything, and I can't believe you, of all people, would accuse me of something as awful as that." She quivered with anger, and paused for a moment to collect herself before continuing in a low voice. "I am quite happy with my life, thank you very much, and I honestly cannot think of any hopes and dreams I've had to sacrifice, except the usual childhood ones of being the next Nancy Drew."

"What about your ice-skating?" Lucy fixed her with a beady stare. "You were so talented, and you loved skating."

Natasha blinked in surprise. She had not thought about that for years. "Well, yes, I did love skating, but it was never going to be a career. And—"

"Talking of which, what about your dreams of being a museum curator?" Another large swallow of wine punctuated Lucy's words. "You can't possibly tell me that working in a school office is your dream job."

"How many people do you know who end up doing their *dream job*, Aunt Lucy? Very few, I'm sure."

Irritation sharpened Natasha's voice. "And as for not committing myself to a relationship, I would prefer to actually find someone I want to spend the rest of my life with, rather than marrying the first man who happens to show an interest."

She was visibly shaking at the end of her quiet outburst, and she pushed her chair back from the table. "If you will excuse me, I need a little fresh air."

She turned and stalked from the room, grateful for the fact that both Nicky and Kyle were still engrossed in their game.

****

It was a beautiful, cloudless night and, as Natasha made her way to the sun deck, the cool breeze against her burning face was a welcome relief. Stars crowded the velvety black sky, shining more brightly than she had ever seen, but she was wound too tightly to appreciate them.

Resting her forearms on the railing, she lowered her head onto her arms, sighing deeply and trying to calm her racing thoughts. She had been completely unprepared for Lucy's outburst, and her stomach squirmed in response to the unexpected argument. She didn't mind Lucy's comments about her job so much; it was something that had been occupying Natasha's thoughts more recently anyway. Over the last few months — since she had split up with Paul, if she were honest — she had been reflecting on a possible change of career.

Her parents' death when she was just eighteen years old had meant looking for a job if she was going to support herself and Nicky, who was still at school. Any plans she may have had to go to university were out of the question. A job at one of the local schools allowed her to be at home during the holidays, and had been ideal. Natasha enjoyed the work and had since progressed to become the school business manager, but now it was time to move on, time to really look for something that she wanted to do. This holiday had been a part of that first step to finding herself, breaking out of her usual habit of planning and organising everything down to the last detail.

No, Lucy's words about giving up her dreams of a museum curatorship didn't bother her. What hurt was her aunt accusing her of using Nicky as an excuse to not get involved with anyone, of being a martyr. That was unfair, and it really stung.

Footsteps on the deck interrupted her troubled thoughts and she stiffened, straightening up immediately, unwilling to let her aunt know how deeply those words had cut.

"Are you all right?" The deep voice belonged to Kyle, and she snapped around in surprise to see him standing a pace away, offering her a glass.

"Yes, I'm fine." She frowned slightly, thrown by his apparent concern. She automatically took the proffered glass. "Thank you."

There was a moment of silence, and she took a swallow of the wine, mainly for something to do.

"Did Lucy send you up here?" She was unable to think of any other reason why he might follow her.

For a moment she thought he was going to ignore her, when he simply looked at her with the assessing gaze that was becoming familiar, the one that made her insides quiver. However, when she moved uneasily, he gave a faint smile and shook his head. He moved to the railing, unconsciously mirroring her earlier stance.

"No. Fortunately, Lucy is completely oblivious to any offence or hurt she may have caused by that rather surprising outburst." A sudden noise from the riverbank on the far side of the Nile broke the stillness of the evening, and drew his gaze. The flapping of wings and harsh cries as several birds took to the night skies, revealed the source. "Don't judge her too harshly. She's concerned about you."

Natasha felt again that quick stab of irritation; who was he to tell her what her aunt was feeling? Deciding it was probably wise to keep her mouth shut, she allowed the silence between them to lengthen once more.

"Have you thought that perhaps the reason you were so upset is because there was an element of truth to Lucy's words?" Kyle continued to stare out over the water for a few more seconds before turning his gaze to her.

"So, you're a psychologist now?" She could hardly believe what she was hearing. To hell with giving him the benefit of the doubt; this man was insufferable. "Have you thought that perhaps you should keep your opinions to yourself? Particularly opinions on a subject about which you know absolutely nothing."

She lifted her chin defiantly when he straightened to lean back against the railing, one eyebrow slightly raised, and a faint smile curving his lips.

"Seems like I touched a nerve."

"You know nothing about me, Kyle Richardson," she hissed, leaning closer to reinforce the point. He returned her gaze with an air of amusement, before dropping his eyes to her mouth, inches from his own.

Natasha stepped back as if she had been stung. "If

you'll excuse me, I think I'll call it a night."

For the second time that day, she turned and walked away from the man who was quickly becoming an instant source of irritation.

Chapter Three

Kyle poured himself a whisky before settling down on the sofa in the salon and closing his eyes, the sound of Bach's Brandenburg Concerto Number Five softly filling the room. He couldn't remember the last time he had been part of any sort of social gathering; nowadays he preferred his own company. Not that he hadn't enjoyed this evening. In fact, it had brought home just how much he missed being part of a group of family or friends. Witnessing the close relationship shared by Natasha and her brother, he had been slightly envious of their easy manner and the almost subliminal messages that passed between the pair. But now that everyone had retired for the evening, he relished this quiet time for reflection, and found himself relaxing and enjoying being back on the *Aten's Dream*.

His thoughts drifted back to earlier that evening, to the conversation with Natasha, and he smiled reluctantly. She was a feisty one, but he could see that her defiance and quick temper hid a softer, more vulnerable side. He had followed her out on the deck with the intention of making sure she was all right after Lucy's outburst, but was at a loss to explain why he had then been deliberately argumentative. Did he enjoy the banter? He couldn't deny the lick of desire that had shot through him when she leaned towards him in anger, her eyes flashing dangerously. In that moment, he had wanted to kiss her.

The door handle gave a soft squeak as someone in the corridor outside slowly opened the door, obviously trying to make as little noise as possible. Unsettled by his thoughts, Kyle was almost relieved by the intrusion, until he realised it was Natasha. He sat quite still when she padded into the room, her bare feet making almost no sound on the polished wooden floor.

He was aware of a sudden dryness in his throat as he gazed at her unobserved; her short-sleeved cotton robe hung open to reveal a white vest top and shorts, and long, slender legs. She carefully closed the door behind her, and he saw the moment she became aware of the soft music because she froze, turning around slowly and gasping in surprise when she saw him sitting on the sofa at the opposite end of the room. She hesitated, and he could see her debating whether or not to stay.

"I'm sorry, did the music wake you?" he said.

"No, no, I didn't hear a thing. I couldn't sleep." She shook her head, fingers resting on the door handle. "I didn't mean to disturb you. I was just going to get a bottle of water."

"You're not disturbing me. I couldn't sleep either." He gestured with his glass to the other sofa set at right angles to his. "Have a seat."

"Oh no, I'll get the water, and leave you to it."

The subdued lighting in the salon bounced off her glossy dark hair, tousled from having tossed and turned in bed, and he suddenly found himself wanting her to stay. "Bottled water isn't going to help your insomnia, but perhaps my company might bore you enough to send you to sleep."

After a moment's hesitation, she gave a shrug and walked across to the sofa. He was unable to prevent his gaze from dropping to her bare legs, and grinned when she snatched the robe around her, tying the belt tightly around her waist and throwing him a look of irritation as she did so.

"Is it the heat?"

Settling into the sofa, she looked at him quizzically.

"Why you couldn't sleep," he elaborated. "Is it too hot in your cabin?"

"Oh." Her brow cleared and she shook her head. "No, not at all. The ceiling fan keeps it pretty cool. I don't know why, but I just don't seem to be all that tired."

"Brooding over your aunt's words, perhaps? Wondering how much truth there was in them?"

"I knew it," she muttered, pushing herself up from the sofa and staring at him coldly. "You can't help yourself, can you?"

He sighed and closed his eyes briefly, annoyed with himself, before reaching out to catch her arm as she stalked past him. She stopped, but stared resolutely across the room.

"I'm sorry," he said softly, his thumb gently caressing the sensitive skin of her inner arm. "That was uncalled for. Stay…please."

She looked down to his hand on her forearm and he saw her swallow, noted a hint of colour appear across her cheeks, and wondered what was going through her head. After a moment, she pulled her arm slowly from his grasp and returned to the sofa, a slight frown marring her brow when she glanced across at him.

Kyle returned her gaze, aware of a sudden spark in the air between them, but determined to ignore it. "Whisky?"

"No, thank you. I'm not keen." She shook her head, wrinkling her nose.

"Joe's niece, not a whisky drinker?" He raised his eyebrows, setting down his glass and moving across to the bar. "Joe always said there was a whisky out there for everyone; the trick was finding the right one."

He stood looking over the bottles shining in the lamplight, before reaching for one bottle in particular, and pouring a splash into a crystal tumbler.

"Here, try this one."

"I really don't think…"

"Just try it," he insisted softly.

With a little sigh, Natasha took the glass from him and lifted it gingerly to her nose. She breathed in, but immediately turned her face away with a grimace.

"Wait." He picked up his own glass before sitting down next to her. "It's a single malt, distilled in the Highlands of Scotland; very smooth."

"Fascinating. I don't like it."

"You haven't tried it." He smiled at her stubbornness. "Whisky is specific to the region in which it is distilled, taking a lot of its fragrance and taste from the landscape of that region. Whiskies from Islay in Scotland, for example, are smoky and peaty, whereas you should be able to taste hints of vanilla and spices in yours."

When she continued to stare at him dubiously, he raised his own glass to his nose and breathed in several deep breaths. He gestured for her to do the same. After a moment, she shrugged, and lifted the glass to her nose. Once again, she took in the sharp, powerful scent of alcohol and winced, but before she could move the glass away, Kyle's hand closed over hers and held it still. He saw her eyes widen as she met his gaze.

"Give it a moment. Once you get past the smell of alcohol, you'll get to the true fragrance of the whisky."

Obediently, she continued to breathe in slowly, and her eyes narrowed slightly before flicking up to stare at him in surprise. He grinned, enjoying her reaction.

"Tell me what you've got."

"You're right, there is a hint of vanilla and… and yes, spices."

"Good. Now drink it."

She took a sip of the whisky, savouring it on her tongue for a moment before swallowing. She gave a soft, disbelieving laugh.

"Wow, that's actually quite nice."

"A whisky for everyone." He suddenly became aware of her nearness, her knee barely touching his, and his heart began beating a little faster in his chest. Confused by his reaction, he moved back to take his previous seat on the other sofa, forcing himself to smile when Natasha looked at him in surprise.

Half an hour passed with them talking about nothing in particular, both careful to keep the conversation vague, unwilling to engage in another argument. After a while, Kyle noticed her eyelids growing heavy, and he took the opportunity to sit there and simply look at her, marvelling at the length of her eyelashes, long enough to cast a shadow across her cheekbones as her eyes once more fluttered shut. As her head dipped, she looked up quickly, catching him observing her and aware that she had been caught nodding. She frowned slightly and opened her mouth, but he spoke first.

"There's something about you. I just can't put my finger on it." He shook his head slightly, tilting his head to one side. "Something...familiar...like a half-forgotten memory. I don't know. Maybe you've got a look of Lucy somewhere. Maybe that's it." He didn't sound overly convinced.

"Maybe I've got one of those faces." She smiled and gave a shrug, as if uncomfortable under his scrutiny. "Anyway, I'm going to call it a night. I'm not sure if it's the whisky or your conversation, but I'm definitely feeling sleepier."

He raised his eyebrows at her mischievous comment and was totally disarmed when she smiled at him; the whisky had obviously had a relaxing effect upon her. "*Touché*." He nodded his head in acknowledgement of his earlier comment. "Good night, Natasha."

"Good night..."

Kyle's grin widened as he understood her hesitation. Should she call him Kyle or Mr. Richardson following their amicable conversation over the last hour? He was rewarded to see the colour rising along her neck, and she turned away with a scowl, placing her glass on the table before hurrying out of the room.

****

Waking the next morning, Natasha lay for a while enjoying that comfortable feeling halfway between waking and sleeping. After a while, she became aware they were moving; the boat must already be under sail. Snapping her eyes open, she rolled over to glance at her watch on the bedside table, worried she had overslept. Relieved to find it was only half past seven, she fell back against her pillow and stared up at the ceiling, fascinated by the dappled light reflected there from the Nile River.

She allowed herself a few minutes more lazing in bed before reluctantly swinging her feet to the floor, and padding across to the en-suite, where she took a leisurely shower. Dried and dressed, with her damp hair wrapped in a towel, she pushed open the window, and leaned out to look back along the boat for a moment, before withdrawing to sit on the sofa and marvel at the lush green vegetation along the banks of the river as they sailed past.

Sinking back against the cushions, a smile curled her lips and she hugged herself in sudden excitement. She was finally here in Egypt, sailing along the Nile as the pharaohs of old must have done all those thousands of years ago. She had enjoyed the hustle and bustle of Cairo, and been overawed by the pyramids, despite having to battle with claustrophobia within the dark, oppressive confines of the Great Pyramid itself. But this was what she had most been looking forward to, cruising along the river, and stopping off to visit the wonderful temples she had only ever seen in books. Even her dislike of Kyle Richardson had been tempered by the side to him she had seen last night. She allowed herself to be cautiously optimistic, hoping for a ceasefire in the hostilities the two of them had shared so far.

Deciding she had lingered in her room long enough, she shook her hair out from the towel and combed it through. It was still damp, so she left it loose, but snatched up a brightly coloured gauze scarf to tie it back later. In the absence of any pockets in her long, white skirt, she tied the scarf around her wrist for now and made her way into the salon. Despite the early hour, there was already a heavy warmth to the day, warning of the blistering heat yet to come.

****

Kyle looked up as Natasha walked in, seeing her

hesitate for a second when she caught sight of him, before making her way to the same sofa she had occupied last night. As she crossed the room, the early morning sun streamed through the windows, momentarily shining through her thin, cotton skirt, and allowing him another glimpse of those long slender legs. The white camisole top complimented her smooth, golden skin, and he was suddenly aware of the same dryness in his throat that he had experienced last night.

Irritated by his reaction to her presence — *she'd only walked in the room, for God's sake!* — he dragged his gaze from her pretty, bare shoulders, and took a large swallow of black coffee, wincing as it burned its way down his throat.

"Morning." He saw her look at him warily, and was aware that his irritation with himself had made his voice sharper than he intended. He made a deliberate effort to get a grip and gestured with his cup. "There's fresh coffee on the bar, and fruit and yogurt. If you want something hot, I can—"

"No, no, fruit and yogurt is fine."

When she breezed past him, his senses were assailed by her soft, clean fragrance; faint traces of shampoo and soap mingled with the light, floral perfume she wore. He sat motionless, eyes closed, as he struggled to make sense of the feelings she aroused in him; feelings he thought he'd never feel again.

⁂⁂

Natasha took her time choosing grapes, strawberries, and slices of orange, before covering them in yogurt. There was also a basket full of fresh pastries, and she helped herself to a croissant before pouring herself a coffee. Balancing the croissant precariously on top of her fruit, she carried the bowl and coffee cup back to the sofa but, instead of sitting down, hesitated in indecision.

Kyle raised his eyebrows, and she blushed slightly.

"I…er…I thought I might have breakfast up on the sun deck?"

He shrugged and waved his hand dismissively. "Eat your breakfast where you like."

She nodded and turned away with something close to relief, but came to a halt when she reached the closed door, looking around for somewhere to put her coffee cup so she could open it. Turning around, she came face to face with Kyle, and she jumped in surprise. He leaned close to reach past her for the door handle.

"Allow me."

She ignored the sarcastic tone and simply murmured her thanks. When she reached the stairs leading up to the sun deck, she hesitated once more, biting her lip when she realised that she was likely to stand on the hem of her skirt if she tried climbing the steps with both hands full.

"Would you like me to assist?"

He was standing in the doorway to the salon, leaning against the jamb with his hands folded across his chest. She bristled at his bored tone.

"I can manage…thank you."

"Really?" He sauntered towards her, flicking his gaze insolently from her head to her toes. "I'm afraid I can't risk being sued for compensation should you trip and fall."

Natasha was trying to find a pithy comeback when he took the bowl of fruit and coffee cup from her hands, and made his way up the stairs. She stared at his broad shoulders for a few seconds, seething inside at the ease with which he could irritate her, before grasping her skirt to lift it clear of her feet as she followed him. Her heart sank when she saw him settle himself in one of the wicker chairs; he was obviously intending to stay up here on the sun deck.

Choosing the chair furthest from him, Natasha deliberately ignored Kyle. Ignored the way the tan-coloured slacks moulded to his thighs when he stretched out his legs, crossing them at the ankles; ignored the way his biceps flexed as he folded his arms across his chest. She looked away quickly, and concentrated on pulling apart the wonderfully tasty, buttery croissant. As the pastry melted on her tongue, she realised how hungry she was and quickly finished the rest before reaching for her bowl of fruit.

"We should reach Beni Suef around ten o'clock this morning," he suddenly said conversationally. She saw his gaze drop to her mouth, his eyes narrowing when she delicately licked yogurt from the back of her spoon. "It's a twelve-hour sail from Cairo, but we made good headway yesterday, so we should have time to explore the city. There's quite a good museum there. We'll come back to the boat for lunch and then, once the worst of the heat is over, we can go across to the pyramid at Meidum."

"I'd like that. It sounds good."

She smiled at him with genuine pleasure, and his eyes widened in surprise before he took a breath, his Adam's apple rising and falling as he swallowed. Her smile faded when their eyes met and held for the longest moment; her heart pounded uncomfortably in her chest, and she wondered at this unexpected chemistry that existed between them.

A sudden clattering on the stairs broke the spell and she dropped her head, leaning forward to place her empty bowl on the table. Nicky appeared on the sun deck and flung himself on the chair beside her.

"Hi!"

"Morning, sleepyhead." She relaxed back into her chair, glad of the interruption. "You slept well, then?"

"Oh, I've been up for ages," he grinned, fidgeting with his usual excitement. "I've been in the…gal…gallery…with Mahmoud and Nader."

"The galley?" She gently corrected him. "I see. So, what have you been up to?"

"Well, Kyle was asking me what you usually ate for breakfast, so I went down to the kitchen…I mean galley…and had a look to see what he'd got." Nicky smiled proudly at being asked for his help. "I told him you usually ate that rabbit food stuff, but he didn't have any, so I said you also liked fruit and yogurt, and boring things like that. He wasn't sure if we had any yogurt, but Mahmoud found some. I made sure that I washed the fruit in bottled water as well, so you don't get sick. Mahmoud told me that you have to wash everything in bottled water, if you're not used to everything here."

Surprised that Kyle seemed to have tried to prepare a breakfast to her taste, she shot him a glance but found his expression unreadable.

"I see. Sounds like you had fun. So have you had your breakfast then?"

"Yep! I showed Nader how to make my special scrambled eggs." He leaned forward as if to impart a secret. "I think he was quite impressed. He said he'd never seen scrambled eggs with honey before."

She couldn't help but laugh. Ever since he was little, Nicky had enjoyed the rather odd combination of scrambled eggs with a drizzle of honey. She could well imagine Nader's face when he saw Nicky rustling up his favourite breakfast.

"I hope you cleaned away after yourself. I know what my kitchen looks like after you've been in it."

"I did, I promise." He turned to Kyle. "You liked my special scrambled eggs, didn't you?"

Kyle gave a slow smile, unintentionally sending Natasha's pulse racing. "It was certainly an interesting combination." He pushed himself to his feet. "Well, I'd better go down and see how Mahmoud is getting on."

"Oh, can I come with you?"

Nicky leapt to his feet and looked beseechingly at Kyle, but Natasha spoke up quickly. "Nicky, Mr. Richardson is busy, and so are Nader and Mahmoud. You need to let them get on with their work."

"It's fine, it's not a problem." Kyle smiled at Nicky and waved his hand to suggest that he should go first. He turned back to Natasha with a raised eyebrow. "Unless, of course, it's a problem for you?"

"No, of course not."

She watched them make their way down the stairs, unconsciously biting her lip, but was saved from worrying about Nicky's apparent attachment to Kyle by the appearance of Lucy on the sun deck. She obviously had no recollection of her outburst last night, and settled in her chair quite happily with the comment that she had slept like the dead. Nader was the next to appear, carrying a tray with fresh coffee, including an extra cup for Natasha, a selection of pastries, and more fresh fruit.

Somewhat older than Mahmoud, Nader presented a

calm, peaceful presence, and Natasha could imagine that he had not been at all perturbed by Nicky's rather chaotic approach to cooking in the kitchen. He carefully set the tray on the small coffee table and asked if Lucy required anything else.

"No thank you, Nader. Everything looks absolutely lovely."

The serene Egyptian beamed at Lucy and gave a short bow before disappearing once more below deck.

The two women spent a pleasant hour watching the world pass by slowly as the boat made its way along the Nile, occasionally talking, but more often sitting in companionable silence, and Natasha felt her heart lift with the pleasure of it all.

As Kyle had predicted, it was around half past ten that morning when she was stirred from her reverie by shouts coming from the bank. She saw Kyle leap easily from the boat to tie it up against the mooring, and sat forward in sudden excitement. They had arrived at their first destination.

Chapter Four

Kyle had pre-arranged for transport to be waiting for them, and as she bounced around in the Jeep, Natasha gazed through the windows in anticipation, trying to catch her first glimpse of the pyramid. Earlier, she had spent an enjoyable morning exploring the pretty city of Beni Suef which, with its large mansions of white brick and red tiled roofs and green structured gardens, had rather oddly reminded her more of Eastern Europe than Egypt.

The driver had dropped them off outside the museum, where Natasha, Lucy and Nicky had enjoyed wandering around and learning about the city's history. Of more interest to the three tourists, however, were the floors dedicated to the many artefacts and relics found at nearby archaeological sites. Kyle had not joined them that morning, instead murmuring something about needing to run a few errands and that he would see them back by the Jeep in a couple of hours.

Following lunch on the dahabeeyah, Lucy elected to remain on the boat rather than drive out to the pyramid at Meidum, so it was just the three of them now making their way along the long, dusty road.

And then, all of a sudden, there it was. The Meidum pyramid.

They were still many miles away, but it was an impressive sight nonetheless; a large, squat structure, seemingly standing alone on the edge of the desert. It was the most un-pyramid-like building Natasha had ever seen, but even so her heart began thumping in excited anticipation.

Next to her, in the back of the Jeep, Nicky was leaning towards Kyle in the front seat, talking ten to the dozen, as he had been doing from the moment they set off. Taking out her mobile phone, Natasha tapped the camera application and snapped a shot of her brother just as Kyle turned his head to respond to something Nicky had said. Their eyes met for an instant and she saw an amused sort of helplessness as he attempted to get a word in edgeways.

She touched Nicky's shoulder, stopping him in mid-flow. "Hey, how about giving Kyle a couple of minutes' peace?"

"Oh, okay." Not bothered in the slightest, Nicky sat back in his seat, and turned his attention to the landscape outside.

****

Twenty minutes later they pulled to a stop in the makeshift car park and, alighting from the Jeep, Natasha was at once struck by the heat of the Egyptian sun, in stark contrast to the cool, air-conditioned interior of the vehicle. It took a few moments for her to get used to breathing in the warm, arid air.

The pyramid rose up before them, surrounded by and sitting on top of a huge mound of stone debris, proof that at one time this pyramid had worn an outer casing that would have rendered the sides smooth and straight. The towering structure reminded Natasha more of a giant wartime bunker than a pyramid, but she was keen to begin exploring. As Nicky came to stand beside her, she linked her arm through his, and they headed towards the path leading to a rather rickety-looking gate, where they found the obligatory site attendant squatting on his haunches to one side.

"Natasha." Kyle's soft voice halted her in her tracks, and she turned back to see him holding out her wide-brimmed straw hat. "You'll need this. There's still a lot of heat in that sun."

She had forgotten all about her hat in her excitement to see the pyramid. Now she took it gratefully from his grasp. "Thank you."

He fell into step beside them as they paid the entrance fee and began exploring the site. When she expressed surprise that there were no other tourists around, he explained that Meidum was not one of the more popular destinations — a point he personally felt was a shame — and that tourism in general had not yet recovered from the recent political troubles in Egypt.

Originally over ninety metres high, only the first three layers of the pyramid were now visible, and Kyle led them through the entrance and down a long corridor, which gradually descended lower. Natasha was grateful for Kyle's earlier advice that she should change into trousers before setting off; access to some of the internal chambers was only possible via a rickety wooden ladder. Fortunately, the corridors themselves were well lit, and high enough for them to walk relatively easily, only requiring them to stoop slightly in certain places.

****

Sometime later, having exhausted the pyramid and the small funerary temple on the eastern side, Nicky settled himself down on one of the low walls and started sketching, finding a willing subject in the rather scruffy-looking local attendant.

"What's that over there?" Natasha shielded her eyes from the sun, squinting at what appeared to be another set of tombs.

"Are you up for an adventure?" Kyle smiled at her. "Those tombs are not for the faint-hearted. It involves a fair amount of crawling around in the dark, but it's worth the effort."

"Oh, I don't know. I'm not that good with enclosed spaces. Maybe not." Wrinkling her nose, she shook her head in disappointment. "The pyramid there was about as tight as I can manage, I think."

He caught her hand in his, and pulled her gently towards the roughly-hewn entrance. "Come on, you'll be fine. I'll be with you every step of the way. You'll regret it if you don't at least give it a go."

"Yes! Yes! Is good. You go. Yes!"

She turned in surprise to see the attendant nodding his head enthusiastically and waving his hands in the direction of the tombs. His weathered face was wreathed in smiles, showing a set of badly decayed teeth, but his meaning was clear; she should go to the tombs.

"Tash, will you just go? I can't draw him when he's waving his arms around like that." Nicky didn't look up from his drawing, his pencil flying across the page as he tried to capture his moving subject.

"Will you trust me?" Kyle asked softly, his fingers gently squeezing hers where they rested in his hand.

Lifting her clear, green eyes to his dark sapphire gaze, she realised that, at that moment, she would probably have agreed to walk barefoot across hot coals had he asked her to…just so long as he continued to hold her hand.

"Okay."

****

She began to regret such romantic notions almost the moment they crossed the threshold to the entrance, which had originally been made by tomb robbers, Kyle informed her. The short corridor sloped down towards a small shaft, where a wooden ladder led to another tunnel. This tunnel was dimly lit and very hot, with little air.

Natasha could feel her breathing become laboured, and her heart began to beat rapidly in her chest as Kyle continued to hold her hand, keeping up a running commentary of the history attached to these tombs, perhaps in an attempt to take her mind off the claustrophobic surroundings. But when they reached the end of the tunnel, her heart sank to her boots when she saw the small hole in the bottom of the wall. She held up a hand as if to ward him off as she inched backwards along the tunnel.

"No. No. You can't expect me to go through there."

Kyle gave her an assessing glance, his expression softening when he observed her obvious unease.

"Hey," he said softly, reaching out for her. "It's just a short crawl… You're so slim you won't even touch the sides."

She shook her head and shrugged herself free from his grasp. "No, it's too small, Kyle."

"Natasha, listen to me." His voice was soft but insistent. "It's a short crawl, and then it opens out into a large passageway and the entrance to the burial chamber. It's beautiful, and you'll love it. I promise."

She stood beside him, breathing heavily and trying desperately to overcome her fear, gazing as if transfixed at the seemingly impossibly small hole cut into the uneven stone wall.

After a moment he touched her shoulder. "Look forget it, it doesn't matter." He ducked his head to smile at her. "I shouldn't have insisted you come down here. This is meant to be an adventure, not a trial, and you don't have to do anything you're not comfortable with. Come on."

When he started back down the tunnel, Natasha tugged at his hand, and he turned back to her with an enquiring frown. Struggling to control her uneven breathing, she searched his eyes for signs of disappointment in her, but was unable to read anything in his gaze. "Will you go first?"

He shook his head. "No, you first. But I'll be right behind you, I promise."

"What if I get stuck?" Her voice quavered as she stared at him.

"You won't get stuck. Believe me, I've done this many times, and there's quite a bit more bulk to me than you." He smiled and gave her a gentle shove towards the hole. "No more talking. Come on, let's do it."

Natasha swallowed hard and took a deep, calming breath before tentatively stooping low and easing herself into the narrow tunnel. No sooner had her feet left the floor as she crawled forwards, than she could feel herself beginning to panic. The narrow space was more than big enough for her to crawl through with a couple of inches to spare around her shoulders and hips, but it was still tight, and the air was acrid and stale.

As she inched forwards, one shoulder grazed the roof, and she suddenly felt as if the walls were narrowing in around her. She stopped immediately, squeezing her eyes shut while her heart slammed painfully against her ribcage.

"Keep calm, you can do this," she whispered over and over, trying to draw in a deep breath to slow down her heartrate. Her movements had disturbed the sandy dust lining the floor, and it caught in the back of her throat, making her cough and gasp and breathe in more of the hot dusty air. She began to shuffle backwards in fear.

"I can't do it. It's too small, I can't breathe." Her voice echoed around her, and she gave a panicked cry when she felt Kyle's hands on her boots, preventing her from moving backwards any further.

"Yes, you can. It's fine, there's plenty of room and plenty of air."

"Kyle, let go. Let me out!" Her muffled voice floated back to him.

"No, keep going. I'm coming in after you."

She felt his hands shove her forwards and she scrambled quickly with the momentum, hearing him crawling in behind her. As he continued to shove at her boots, keeping her moving, Natasha found her fear receding as her irritation grew. Almost before she knew it, her head cleared the entrance to the much larger passageway and she tumbled out in relief, landing in a somewhat ungainly heap on the sandy floor. Seconds later, Kyle's dusty head appeared, and he eased himself out of the crawl space.

"See, wasn't so bad, was it?" He grinned at her as he ran a hand through his hair.

"I didn't have much choice, did I?" She turned away from him when his grin widened, irritation burning in her stomach.

"Hey, you faced your fear." His voice was suddenly

gentle, and he turned her around to face him. "You did really well. I'm proud of you."

Her anger dissipated as suddenly as it had appeared and, although her heart continued to beat wildly in her chest, she was no longer sure if it was simply due to the confined space she had just crawled through.

"And now for your reward." He clasped her hand in his once more and led her down the passage, stopping halfway along where the entrance to the burial chamber was located.

****

It was a large, impressive chamber hewn entirely from limestone, and Natasha gasped when she saw the granite sarcophagus still in its final resting place at the end of the chamber. She followed Kyle when he motioned for her to crouch down at the side of the massive tomb, pointing out the lid which had been pushed to one side by tomb robbers thousands of years before. She followed his gaze and caught her breath when she saw the small, wooden object jammed between the sarcophagus and the lid.

"What is it?" she whispered.

"It's a wooden mallet, left by the tomb robbers when they plundered this tomb."

"Oh Kyle, that's amazing." Natasha stared at the ancient little hammer, trying to imagine the grunts and groans of the robbers as they heaved aside this granite lid by flickering torchlight all those years ago.

"So, was it worth it?"

"It was worth it." She returned his smile and for a moment fought the urge to fling her arms around his neck, instead turning away and pretending to inspect the rest of the chamber.

****

Half an hour later, they emerged from the dim, oppressive tombs, blinking in the dazzling brightness of the sun sitting high in the pale, cloudless sky. Natasha breathed in huge gulps of the clean, fresh air, for the moment hardly minding that it was uncomfortably warm. She had thrust herself into that awful crawl space at speed, trying to get through it as quickly as possible without thinking and without Kyle's 'helpful' shoves this time, but still it had left her sweating and breathless, her heart racing in fear.

Nevertheless, she was left feeling elated; she had done it. And, oh, what a reward! Not only had the burial chamber been amazing, with the little wooden mallet forming a bridge right back to the day the tomb had been robbed, but she could also not forget Kyle's proud smile when she had conquered her fear.

She ran across to where Nicky was sitting in the shade of a small building, now sketching the pyramid itself. She came to a stop in front of him, beaming with happiness at her recent adventure. He looked up at her and smiled.

"Hi Tash. Was it good? Why are you all dusty?"

****

Kyle stared out across the Nile, for once gaining little comfort from the gentle lapping of the water against the hull of the boat, or the golden dappled ripples reflecting the sun as it sank lower in the sky. His thoughts were full of Natasha, of the triumphant expression that lit her eyes when she'd emerged from that narrow crawl space. Her face had been dusty and her hair escaping from the equally dusty scarf to fall in tendrils across her cheekbones, but she had never looked more beautiful, and he had felt unaccountably proud of her. He wondered at that; wondered at the depth of feelings this woman seemed to arouse in him. And he had a vague sense of uneasiness.

He recalled how her face had shone in the muted lamplight when he explained the pyramid's history, and it was with some surprise that he'd found his spirits being lifted by her enthusiasm and excitement. Over the many years he had studied Egyptology, and certainly over the last five years, he had somehow lost his wonder for this country and its history. Now he found himself experiencing it all over again through Natasha's eyes, falling in love once again with the genius of the ancient Egyptian people.

He blew out a long, irritated sigh. This wasn't what he wanted; wasn't part of the plan. He should know better than to let his guard down. He didn't mind a bit of fun now and again, but this felt different; she felt different, and he wasn't prepared for that. He shook his head in frustration and turned around to lean back against the railing, arms folded across his chest.

He blinked in surprise when he saw Natasha walking across the deck towards him. He had not heard her come up the steps, and struggled to retain his composure as his gaze took in the newly washed hair, once again hanging loose, and the sleeveless dress that set off her golden shoulders. The softly draping material that fell to her feet might have been considered demure but, on Natasha, it hinted at soft, sensual curves.

"Hi." She came to within a few steps of him, and stopped somewhat uncertainly. "Um…am I interrupting?"

He shook his head, unwilling to trust his voice at that

moment. She stiffened slightly, and he was aware that his non-verbal response was not particularly welcoming.

"Right. Well, I just…I wanted to thank you for today." Her smile faltered at his continued silence, and she started to say more but obviously thought better of it and, in the end, simply nodded. As she turned to leave, a gust of wind whipped her hair across her face and she automatically brushed it away, pulling the scarf from around her wrist to begin tying her hair back as she walked across the deck.

Kyle closed his eyes, wishing he didn't want her so badly, but looked up when he heard her give a muffled exclamation. She had stopped halfway across the floor and was struggling with her hair.

"What is it?" he asked eventually.

"It's nothing," she said over her shoulder. "I've…oh, my stupid hair has got caught in my stupid watchstrap."

That brought an amused smile to his face, and he chuckled softly at her outburst. "Come here. Let me have a look."

"No, it's…" She continued to struggle, but her hair was caught behind her ear, and she couldn't see to free it. "Oh, for goodness sake!"

"Come here."

Muttering under her breath, Natasha gave up and walked back to Kyle, avoiding his gaze, clearly embarrassed by having to walk with her hand caught behind her ear. He pulled her close, breathing in her familiar perfume, and taking his time to gently tease her hair free of the watch.

"There, all done."

She turned towards him, eyes downcast and cheeks

burning. "Thank you." She immediately reached up to tie back her hair once more, but Kyle pulled the scarf from her fingers.

"It looks pretty when its loose." His fingers brushed a wayward strand of hair from her face, tucking it behind her ear, before moving to the nape of her neck. He gently lifted her chin, raising her eyes to meet his gaze, and his breath caught in his throat when her eyes locked with his.

God, he wanted to kiss her.

"I'm glad you enjoyed today," he said softly, before giving in to temptation and dropping his head to brush his lips against hers. He shook with the effort it required not to fold her into his arms and kiss her senseless, but still he couldn't help but drop another soft kiss on her mouth.

Taking him by surprise, she slipped her hands up over his arms to cup the back of his neck, and her mouth moved against his, kissing him back without hesitation. That was all it took, and he pulled her closer, one hand at her waist, drawing her into him, the other buried in the soft tangles of her hair. Her body was moulded against his and, when he ran his fingers along the curve of her hip, he could feel himself losing control. Reluctantly, he began to draw back, his kiss becoming gentle, and his arms easing around her waist as he lifted his mouth from hers.

He looked down at her, her face only inches from his, and saw her eyes wide and disbelieving. His lips curved in a half smile, and he lifted a hand to draw his fingertips along her cheekbone. He swallowed, not entirely convinced his voice wouldn't break. "Natasha, I—"

They both jumped at the sound of someone running

up the stairs, and Kyle immediately stepped away from her, looking expectantly across the deck. But seconds later, his jaw dropped when he saw who emerged at the top of the stairs.

"Kyle Richardson, as I live and breathe. And how long were you going to leave it before you told me you were back in town?"

Chapter Five

The slim, petite blonde ran across the sun deck and flung herself into Kyle's arms, before planting a lingering kiss on the same lips which, only seconds earlier, had been kissing Natasha so thoroughly.

He stood frozen in shock for a moment before overcoming his surprise and politely disentangling the woman's arms from around his neck, pulling away from her. He was only partially successful, because she immediately slipped her arms around his waist to rest her cheek against his chest.

"Gemma, what are you doing here?" He frowned down at the blonde head pressed against his chest. "How did you know where I was?"

She lifted her head and gave a tinkling laugh, which didn't quite reach her eyes as they fixed on Natasha. "I heard on the grapevine that you were back and, well, I happened to be passing and saw the *Aten's Dream* and thought I'd pop in to see you."

Kyle grasped her arms and held her away from him, ignoring her pretty pout. "You just happened to be passing? You'll forgive me if I don't believe you."

"Oh, Kyle," she reproached playfully. "You're being very rude. You haven't even introduced me to this lovely lady."

He gave an irritated sigh before turning to Natasha. "Natasha, this is a friend of mine, Gemma. Gemma,

Natasha has chartered the boat for a couple of weeks."

"Oh, you've chartered the boat." She reached out a hand, a friendly smile suddenly lighting up her face. "Well, in that case, I'm pleased to meet you, Natasha."

She turned back to Kyle. "And what do you mean *a friend*?" Gemma sidled up against him once more. "I should think we're rather more than friends, wouldn't you?"

Over the top of Gemma's head, Kyle saw Natasha blink in surprise, her gaze lifting to meet his in silent accusation. Dammit. This was turning into a nightmare.

"Don't change the subject," he said, deliberately folding his arms. "You didn't answer my question: what are you doing here?"

"Oh Kyle, why are you being such a bore?" Gemma's seductive pout turned sulky. "What sort of a welcome is this? I thought we could catch up. I've nothing planned over the next few weeks. How about I join you on your little cruise down the Nile?"

He frowned, completely thrown by her suggestion, and uncomfortably aware of Natasha's quiet intake of breath.

"I'm sure Natasha won't mind. It's not as if I'll be taking up an extra cabin, is it?" Once again, she reached her arms around his waist, slipping her hands into his back pockets as she pressed close, looking up at him from beneath her lashes.

"Natasha has chartered the boat, Gemma," said Kyle eventually, when he was sure he could answer her politely. "And I don't believe even you would have the front to invite yourself on her holiday."

"Oh, I won't get in the way, Natasha," smiled Gemma brightly. "You won't even know I'm here."

Natasha hadn't moved throughout the entire conversation, but jumped slightly in surprise when Gemma addressed her directly. Her eyes flickered briefly with an unreadable emotion before she smiled brightly with a glance which encompassed both of them, but somehow managed to avoid Kyle's searching gaze. "This is your boat, Kyle. It's entirely up to you, of course."

"There, I told you so." Gemma laughed triumphantly, seemingly unaware that his gaze had never once wavered from Natasha's face.

"Well, you two must have a lot of catching up to do, so I'm sure you'll excuse me." Natasha nodded politely; her bright smile fixed in place as she quickly left the sun deck.

Kyle stared after her, wanting more than anything to call her back, but Gemma still clung to him. Suddenly unable to bear her arms around him any longer, he took hold of her wrists and firmly disentangled himself from her embrace.

****

"Tash!" Nicky was playing patience with a well-thumbed deck of cards when she walked slowly into the salon area. "Where've you been? You said you were going to have a quick shower and that was ages ago."

Natasha gazed at him blankly for a moment, her mind still racing with thoughts of Kyle and Gemma. "Sorry, Nicky, I was…" Her voice faded away as she came to a halt in the middle of the room.

"Miles away, obviously." Lucy put down her book with an amused smile. "Anywhere nice?"

Natasha's gaze slowly focused on her aunt, and she pointed over her shoulder with her thumb. "I was just…er…well, Kyle…" Unable to construct a meaningful sentence, she let her hand drop to her side.

"What on earth is the matter?" Lucy frowned at her.

Natasha shook her head in annoyance, took a deep breath and tried again. "Kyle's girlfriend is up on the sundeck. I…um…I think she's going to be staying for a few days."

"Kyle's girlfriend?" Lucy leaned forward in pleased surprise, holding a hand to her ample bosom. "Oh Natasha, really? Well, it's about time, too. Joe and I were so worried about him after Carrie, you know. I didn't think he'd ever settle down again, but oh, I'm so pleased."

Suddenly filled with an awful sense of foreboding, Natasha sank into the chair opposite her aunt, and tried to look only mildly interested. "Carrie? Who is she?"

"Well, his wife, of course."

"Kyle is married?" Her stomach gave a disconcerting roll, making her feel slightly nauseous.

"Well, no, not anymore—"

Before Lucy could finish, the door burst open, and Kyle strode in alone. His gaze took in the two women sitting close together with matching guilty expressions, and his face darkened. It wouldn't take a genius to know they'd been talking about him.

Nicky looked up immediately and began shuffling his cards. "Kyle, will you play a game with me? Those two are being boring."

Kyle stopped halfway across the room, in much the same place where Natasha had halted a few minutes before. He took a deep calming breath before turning to her brother and giving him a tight smile. "I'm sorry, Nicky, maybe later.

"Enjoying a good gossip, are we?"

"We're hardly gossiping, Kyle. Natasha was just telling me about your girlfriend," said Lucy, with a frown. "I'm not sure why you're so irritable. It's wonderful news. Is she going to be joining us?"

His gaze flicked from Lucy to Natasha, his face expressionless. "No, Gemma will not be joining us. I'll go and see what's keeping dinner."

With that, he stalked from the room, leaving all three of them staring after him in puzzled surprise.

"Well!" Lucy sniffed and picked up her book. "It would appear they've had a lovers' tiff."

****

Natasha gazed out of her cabin window without really taking in the view, her chin resting on her hands. Kyle had been distant and uncommunicative during dinner, and only the fact that Nicky and Lucy had kept up a constant chatter had saved it from the ordeal it might have been. When Kyle disappeared immediately afterwards, Natasha had sought the sanctuary of her room in an attempt to try and calm her racing thoughts.

She mulled over the casual bombshell Lucy had dropped about Carrie, Kyle's obviously 'ex' wife. From what little Lucy had said, it would appear he had been devastated by the break-up of his marriage. Natasha shook her head; it had never occurred to her that he might have a girlfriend, let alone that he might be married.

Why had she assumed that he was single? Perhaps it was the obvious attraction she saw in his glance, although she wasn't naïve enough to imagine that someone in a relationship would never find anyone else attractive. She heaved a sigh and rubbed a hand wearily across her face.

She wished she didn't care and could just enjoy being on holiday, but she couldn't. This was so far from what she had imagined it would be. Lazy mornings spent dozing in the sun as they sailed down the Nile, with afternoons spent exploring ancient temples in the searing heat of the desert. But although the reality had elements of that, overshadowing it all was Kyle Richardson. She had not bargained on such a distraction; someone whose mere presence sent her emotions into turmoil. Try as she might, she could not deny the way her body responded to him, and even more mortifying was the realisation that perhaps the feeling wasn't as mutual as she had imagined.

The arrival of Gemma this evening had turned things around yet again. The woman had made it clear she and Kyle were intimately involved with each other, and Natasha's cheeks burned with embarrassment at the realisation she had read more into his kiss than he had intended. God, what if he had been imagining that she was Gemma or, worse still, his wife, when he had been kissing her? What if he had kissed her simply because she was there and available? She groaned and buried her face in her hands, cringing at the thought.

But why had Gemma not stayed on the boat? It didn't make any sense. Unless she, Natasha, had been unsuccessful in hiding her displeasure at having his girlfriend join them. She sighed heavily. That would certainly explain Kyle's foul temper.

A sudden clatter in the corridor outside interrupted her despondent thoughts, followed by an impatient knocking on her door.

"Come in, Nicky." She smiled, grateful for the distraction.

Nicky flung open the door. "I'm so bored!" He shrugged impatiently and gestured down the corridor. "Aunty Lucy has fallen asleep, I can't find Kyle, and everyone else is busy. Come on, Tash, I want to play cards."

"All right, I'm coming." She shooed him out of her room and followed him back up to the salon where they played cards to the accompaniment of Lucy's soft snoring in the corner.

****

Kyle lay on his bed, staring at the ceiling fan with his arms folded behind his head. The music on his smartphone was turned up as loud as he could stand with his earphones in — a mixture of his favourite operatic arias blasting out and threatening to deafen him. This was his sure-fire way of relaxing, of forcing all thoughts from his head, but tonight it wasn't working. Swearing fluently, he ripped off the earphones, pulled them from his phone, and threw them angrily across the room. He swung his legs off the bed and dropped his head into his hands with a groan.

What in the world was happening to him? A month ago, his life had been so simple; he worked every hour he could, taking short-term consultancy or research posts across Egypt, moving regularly so he didn't have to deal with the inconvenience of maintaining friendships. He already had the only friends he wanted — Nader, Mahmoud, and Lucy — and they understood his need to keep moving, returning 'home' only every now and then. He knew what they thought about his reasons for keeping his distance, but his only concern was to keep them arm's length enough to be safe. Female company was something he sought out rarely and only ever on a casual basis; he didn't want or need anything more complicated than that.

Gemma had suited him for a while, a kindred spirit insistent that she was only looking for a bit of fun, and they had enjoyed a brief fling earlier in the year. But now he frowned, wondering about her sudden appearance. She had made it clear enough tonight that she wanted to pick up where they'd left off. His frown deepened. That was not going to happen. Had he not been clear enough all those months ago that he was not interested in anything more? He shook his head. No, he'd been clear. They had both been clear; in fact, she had been particularly vocal about not wanting any kind of commitment.

He sighed. Maybe he was reading too much into this. What was it Gemma had said? She was in the area and had decided to drop in to see him. As unlikely as that may sound, maybe he just had to take her at her word. He shrugged. It didn't matter now anyway, he had made his feelings clear, and she was gone.

As he reflected on Gemma's sulky pout, he couldn't help but compare her to Natasha. She was probably only a couple of years older than Natasha, but there the similarity ended. The contrast between Natasha's natural beauty and Gemma's heavily made-up face had been surprising to him, never having taken much notice before. He wondered why she needed such a lot of make-up. It was completely impractical in such a hot climate, and it wasn't as if Gemma was lacking in confidence. Hell, it took some gall to invite yourself onto someone else's holiday.

He had a sudden image of Natasha's face as she had listened to Gemma insisting that Kyle let her join them on the boat. He grimaced, pressing the heels of his hands into his eyes in an effort to banish the vision. He remembered the way her eyes had widened slightly in realisation, swiftly followed by the sudden bright smile and hurried exit. He knew the conclusion she had reached, and it twisted his insides to think she had made the assumption he and Gemma were in a relationship, although he could hardly blame her. Gemma had all but spelled it out.

Unwilling to let her remain under that misapprehension for a minute longer, he pushed himself from the bed to stride out of the room, not allowing himself time to wonder why it was so important for Natasha to know there was nothing between Gemma and himself.

****

The light was fading quickly from the sky as he walked across the sun deck, having made a last-minute diversion in order to gather his thoughts and rehearse what he wanted to say. Making his way slowly down the stairs leading to the narrow walkway outside the salon, he could see the internal lights had been switched on. From this vantage point at the bottom of the stairs, he knew the occupants of the salon would not be able to see him through the windows, would only be able to see the salon reflected back at them in the glass.

In contrast, he could see both Natasha and Nicky clearly. They were playing the ridiculous made-up version of Snap which Nicky had tried to teach him yesterday; the one that involved a lot of frantic counting, card placing, and slapping your hand down at seemingly random intervals. As he watched, both of them darted out a hand towards the messy pile of cards on the table in front of them and, through the glass, he heard their voices crying "Snap!" in unison.

Natasha immediately turned to Nicky in mock outrage, clearly accusing her brother of cheating. But the next minute, they both froze, their gaze turning to the corner of the room beyond Kyle's line of sight. He was puzzled for a moment, then guessed that Lucy must be asleep in one of the comfortable chairs at the other side of the salon. After a few seconds, Natasha and Nicky breathed a sigh of relief and relaxed back against the seats; obviously their merriment had momentarily disturbed Lucy but not enough to waken her.

His gaze was fixed upon the two of them, now convulsed in silent giggles like a pair of school children, leaning against each other in easy harmony, and he was suddenly overcome by a wave of loneliness more acute than he had ever known. He longed for the closeness and unconditional love the two of them clearly shared.

Brushing angrily at the sudden dampness on his cheeks, he turned away and, instead of going into the salon, he carried along the walkway and down the stairs into the little seating area beyond the galley. Mahmoud and Nader were there, also playing cards, although the large pile of counters and currency piled in the middle of the table suggested that theirs did not involve shouting "Snap!". They looked up as Kyle strode in, their gaze following his movements when he reached into one of the cupboards to remove a bottle of whisky and a glass.

"Deal me in." He joined them, and placed the bottle deliberately on the table in front of him. It was going to be a long night.

****

Natasha ate her breakfast in peaceful solitude; Lucy

had not yet surfaced from her room, and Nicky, after bolting down a croissant, had gone off in search of Kyle. She had not seen their host this morning, but knew he was up and about because she had heard the rumble of his deep voice as he spoke with Nader and Mahmoud in the galley.

Sinking back in the comfy chair and sipping at her coffee, Natasha was grateful to be alone. She had not slept particularly well last night and was feeling bleary-eyed as a result. Try as she might, she had not been able to dismiss the memory of their kiss or the burning intensity of his gaze as he had pulled her close. Neither had she been able to forget the sudden intrusion of his girlfriend.

Although Kyle had not appeared particularly pleased to see Gemma, Natasha could understand he would feel uncomfortable with having so nearly been caught kissing another woman. Although reluctant to admit it, Natasha could not deny Gemma's sex appeal; but the woman knew it too. She oozed confidence, and was obviously used to getting her own way. Natasha's stomach churned when she remembered the way Gemma had curled her body around Kyle, clearly staking her claim.

Sudden tears filled her eyes, catching her by surprise, and she blinked rapidly, slipping on her sunglasses in case anyone should come up and find her crying. What did she have to cry about? She was on her dream holiday, cruising along the Nile in a beautiful dahabeeyah with the two people she cared about most in the world, and with a guide who was able to take her to sites she would never have been able to arrange herself.

And therein lay the problem, she silently

acknowledged. That same guide also happened to be undeniably handsome, but with seemingly mercurial moods, which in no way prevented her from longing to feel his lips against hers once more. He continually managed to disarm her, allowing her glimpses of a softer side. She could feel herself falling for him in a way she had never felt about Paul, or about anyone for that matter.

Paul was a lovely, gentle man, but although she had enjoyed his company, he had never set her pulse racing. Looking back, she recognised now that there had always been something missing, but she had been content to let things drift along. She had assumed he felt the same, until he had accepted a new job and asked her to go with him.

He had been so hurt, so angry when she refused. Natasha closed her eyes at the memory, guilt flooding through her. But he had not been surprised and it was that, more than anything, which told her she had made the right decision. He had known things weren't right between them, and been braver than she had. He had forced the issue, forced her out of her lethargy.

Initially, Natasha had been thrown by the sudden sense of freedom. Relief, guilt, and confusion swamped her in equal measures. It had taken her a while to come to terms with that sense of freedom, to allow herself to embrace it and to see the break-up as a new start for them both. Set free, she could see their relationship for what it was; a habit borne out of friendship (certainly on her side), and they both deserved more than that.

The feelings Kyle aroused in her simply confirmed it. She wanted someone in her life who set her pulse racing by just being in the same room, whose kisses left her wanting more. As if to prove the point, her stomach quivered as she remembered the burn of Kyle's hand on the small of her back when he pulled her into him.

She bit her lip. Yes, she wanted someone who could make her feel all those things, but she wished it weren't Kyle who made her feel them. He wasn't the right man for her; she needed someone who at least lived in the same country. And what about Nicky? She could see that he, too, had formed an attachment to this man, and that worried her far more. Whereas she knew there was no future for them with Kyle, Nicky was less likely to understand why he would never see his new best friend again once they returned to England.

What to do? She mused, fanning herself gently against the growing warmth of the morning.

What to do?

****

Mahmoud shooed Natasha from the galley when she ventured downstairs mid-morning to cool off a little. The heat was becoming quite unbearable, despite her shorts and vest top. Relieved to find that his reticence of the first evening had now vanished, she asked if she could help him prepare lunch, but he looked shocked, shaking his head vehemently.

"No, no. You relax, Miss Morgan." He waved her away with a friendly smile. "This is your holiday. You must enjoy and relax and do nothing."

"But, really, I don't mind at all. I'd like to help." She protested in vain and, when she mentioned that Nicky often helped in the galley, was gently informed that that was different.

Turning away with a resigned sigh, she walked straight into Kyle, and stumbled backwards in surprise as he came in through the narrow door. He reached out automatically to steady her, and she blinked up at him, attempting to regain her composure. She could feel the warmth of his fingers where they curled around her arms.

"I'm sorry," she managed, after a somewhat breathless pause. "I didn't see you."

"It was my fault." He shook his head with a frown and, belatedly realizing he was gripping her arms, dropped his hands as if he had been burned. "If you'll excuse me."

He gestured towards the galley but made no effort to squeeze past her in the narrow corridor. Natasha saw him swallow and close his eyes briefly, as if biting back irritation.

"I...er...I meant to ask. Are we going to Amarna today?" She tried a bright smile.

"What?"

"I was looking at my guidebook and, well, I wondered if we would be going to Amarna today. It seems to be just a little further on from Beni Suef and I thought..." She trailed off uncertainly. It was obvious he was still angry with her about Gemma; he could barely force himself to be civil to her. Again, that stab of jealousy spiked through her, and she wished his girlfriend had never set foot on the boat. Until that point, they had been getting on so well; too well, perhaps.

"No," he replied shortly. "We're not."

She blinked at his abruptness and bit back an angry retort, relieved by the immediate return of her previous dislike for the man. She stepped aside to let him past, deliberately refusing to look at him, before pulling open the door.

"Natasha." His voice stopped her in her tracks, but

she didn't look back, simply stood looking out on to the deck. "We'll visit Amarna tomorrow, but this afternoon's trip will be worth it...I promise."

After a long pause, she simply nodded without turning, and walked out onto the deck, closing the door quietly behind her.

Damn him. The soft, almost tender way in which he had spoken those last words had floored her, and she had so wanted to remain angry with him. Now she was just angry with herself. She stamped up the stairs, across the sun deck, and pulled a sun lounger under the canopy before flopping down onto it with a heavy sigh and closing her eyes.

Lucy looked up in surprise at her niece's obvious bad mood. "Everything all right, dear?"

"Everything's fine." She reluctantly opened her eyes, but quickly shut them again when Lucy simply raised her eyebrows and returned to her book.

****

"Do you think Aunt Lucy is okay?" Natasha cast a worried glance at Kyle as she hopped out of the Jeep, unable to prevent the automatic gasp of surprise when the full force of the afternoon sun prickled along her bare skin. She saw his eyebrows draw together in a frown, although whether it was in response to her question or simply because she had spoken to him, she couldn't be sure. He had been particularly uncommunicative during the journey here.

"I should think so. Why?"

"Well, I thought she might join us more on our sightseeing. I mean, I know she must have seen them all before, but I thought..."

She was surprised to see an amused smile lifting the

corners of his mouth. "I think Lucy is perhaps finding the company on board a rather more appealing prospect than tramping around the desert in the searing heat." He reached back into the Jeep to retrieve her hat. "Here, you keep forgetting this."

She automatically took the hat from him and forced it on her head, before reaching out to catch his arm as he turned away. "What do you mean?"

Kyle turned to look at her, his eyes holding hers for the longest moment as if he were trying to read her thoughts. He wore his customary uniform of a battered leather hat, tan slacks, dusty work boots, and khaki shirt open at the neck with the sleeves rolled up to the elbows; he looked deliciously masculine, and seemed completely unaffected by the heat of the day. He held her gaze a few seconds longer before slowly and deliberately sliding his sunglasses over his eyes.

"You haven't noticed how well she and Nader seem to be getting on?"

"Come on, you two." Nicky danced from one foot to the other, moving backwards along the rocky path as he urged them to hurry.

"What do you mean?" Natasha repeated, falling into step alongside Kyle when he turned to follow Nicky.

"What do you think I mean?" He threw her a sideways glance.

"What? You think Aunt Lucy and Nader…" She stared at him open-mouthed, completely taken by surprise.

"Well, I'm not saying I think they're having wild, passionate sex." He smiled at the sudden spots of colour appearing on Natasha's cheeks. "But yes, they are certainly enjoying each other's company."

She remained silent, trying to process the information as Kyle lengthened his stride to catch up with Nicky, leaving her dawdling behind.

Lucy and Nader; she certainly hadn't seen that one coming. Not that she had a problem with it. Remembering the tearful conversation they had shared at the very beginning of their holiday, Natasha was pleased her aunt had found companionship, and a smile curved her lips as little pieces of the jigsaw slotted into place. It was true, Nader had been very attentive towards Lucy, and the last few nights, despite dozing in the salon, she had still been up when Natasha and Nicky had retired to bed.

Her smile widened when she remembered Nader nodding to her politely when she passed him in the corridor on her way to her room last night. She had thought nothing of it at the time, but now she realised he had obviously been on his way to join Lucy in the salon.

She shook her head with a soft laugh, wondering how she could have missed it. Glancing up, she hurried down the road to where Nicky and Kyle were waiting impatiently for her by a steep flight of steps at the base of the cliffs leading up to a rock-cut canopy high on the cliff face. As she approached, Kyle glanced at his watch and strode further down the road, and she bit her lip, wondering if they were late for something, although she couldn't imagine what it was they might be late for.

"Where's Kyle gone?" She stopped somewhat breathlessly next to Nicky, and squinted up the steps to the stone canopy, but could see nothing through what seemed to be darkened glass. "And what on earth is that?"

Nicky shrugged and sat down on the bottom step.

"Dunno. And Kyle's gone to find somebody."

Natasha joined her brother on the bottom step, fanning herself gently with her hat, and relieved to find that the cliff face offered a little shade from the relentless sun. They sat in companionable silence, Nicky drawing circles in the sand with the tip of his pencil, until Kyle reappeared a few minutes later with a tall, willowy Egyptian in tow. In direct contrast to the seemingly ancient site attendant they had seen yesterday, this Egyptian had a smooth, unlined face, with bright, brown eyes that sparkled with good humour as he smiled and swept past them in his pristine white galabeya.

Quickly brushing dust from the back of her thin cotton slacks, Natasha looked up in surprise to see Kyle's hand outstretched towards her. She slipped her hand into his, enjoying the feel of his strong fingers closing around hers as they climbed the steps to where the Egyptian was unlocking what Natasha now realised was a pair of smoked glass doors covering the front of the stone canopy. She looked at Kyle in puzzlement, wondering why there would be such a thing several feet up a cliff face, but he simply smiled at her, releasing her hand when the attendant stood back and gestured for them to move closer.

"See, see." The attendant nodded and ushered her forwards.

Moving through the doors, Natasha saw two statues standing in front of the rock face, obviously once incredibly detailed and beautiful, but now unfortunately missing their heads. Above the statues, and carved directly into the cliff face, was a large frieze depicting Egyptian figures with their hands raised to the sky, alongside row upon row of hieroglyphics. She stared at the frieze, instantly recognizing the figures portrayed, and took in the whole scene, gasping for breath when she realised exactly what it was she was looking at. She turned to Kyle and grasped his arm in her excitement.

"Oh my God, Kyle. Is this one of Akhenaten's boundary stelae?"

He nodded, returning her smile, and without thinking, she threw her arms around his neck, hopping from one foot to the other and laughing in surprised delight. His arms closed around her, and she breathed in the citrusy tang of his cologne, before stepping away from him to take in the stela once more.

"I can't believe it," she said, unable to take her eyes from the rock face. "I don't know why, but I didn't expect it to be so big. I always imagined it to be quite small, which is stupid I know, when you think it was to mark the boundary of his city."

She reached into her bag and brought out her camera, but stopped when the attendant gently touched her arm.

"No. No camera." He smiled apologetically. "No camera." He swept his arm wide to indicate that no photography was allowed anywhere on site.

"Oh, right. Sorry." She smiled and nodded to show her understanding, swallowing her disappointment. A quick glance across at Nicky, partially hidden behind Kyle, confirmed that he was, as usual, capturing the scene with his pencil, and she smiled, reassured that she would at least have some record of the stela. She wondered if that, too, was prohibited, and realised that that might be why Kyle was deliberating shielding her brother from the full view of the attendant.

Turning back to the frieze, her gaze sought and

found the familiar figures of Akhenaten and Nefertiti, with their hands held up towards the rays of the sun. Almost without thinking, Natasha mimicked their stance, hands held palm up, arms bent at the elbow, one in front of the other, tilting her face to the sun. The movement caused her hat to drop to the floor, leaving her head bare, her gleaming dark hair secured neatly in a French pleat. The sun itself had cleared the cliffs, and was now shining down with full force through the open glass doors and on to the ledge on which they stood. It burned into her face and palms, and she could easily understand why Akhenaten and his queen had worshipped the sun as their one true God.

The attendant suddenly spoke rapidly, breaking the spell, and she turned to see him pointing at her with an odd, narrow-eyed glance, which might have worried her had it not been accompanied by a slight smile. She saw Kyle turn to look at her and something like recognition lit his eyes.

"That's it. Of course," he said softly, nodding his head and turning to respond to the attendant in his native tongue.

"What did he say?"

Kyle hesitated, his gaze sweeping her face, and smiled before giving her a slightly cryptic answer. "He said *the beautiful one has come, walks the earth once more.*"

Natasha frowned. "The beautiful one has come? That's what the name Nefertiti means, isn't it?" She nodded in understanding. "Right. It's because I was standing like her, wasn't it?"

Kyle didn't respond directly. "There's plenty more to see around here, if you're ready? Even though the majority of the necropolis is of a much later period and into the Roman era, I think you'll find it interesting."

Natasha spent the rest of the afternoon happily wandering around the open-air museum at Tuna el-Gebel and el-Ashmunein, where the crumbling ruins and dry dusty land, littered with fallen and broken pillars, spoke of a site that had once been gloriously impressive. She gazed at the huge baboon-shaped statues that represented the Egyptian God Thoth, who was more usually depicted as an Ibis, while Kyle and Nicky sat in the shade of one of the larger scrub bushes. From what she could tell, Kyle was attempting to answer Nicky's many and varied questions about everything from how hot it might be today, to how many people he thought it must have taken to sculpt one of the statues Natasha was standing next to.

Reaching into her shoulder bag, she took out a bottle of lukewarm water and thirstily drank half its contents, as grateful for the relief to her parched throat as if it had been a glass of ice-cold water from the filter machine.

Wiping her mouth with the back of her hand, she watched Nicky and Kyle; could see, even from this distance, the hero-worship shining from her brother's eyes as Kyle gestured with his hands in response to one of Nicky's questions. Her eyes narrowed thoughtfully. Paul had always been slightly uncomfortable around her brother, had been unable to cope with Nicky's constant chatter. Although he had tried to build a relationship with him, it had always felt forced; another reason why it would never have worked between them. Who would have thought that the man they would both connect with so quickly would be someone they were destined to know for only a short time?

She felt again that wave of fear and helplessness at

the hurt and confusion she sensed Nicky would feel when they returned home, and he never saw Kyle again. The ache in her heart spoke of her own sorrow at the thought of never seeing this man again, but that was something she could deal with. Her brother's pain and distress, however, was something she permanently feared and was forever mindful of. Determined to be proactive, she made a mental note to speak to Kyle about trying to keep a little more distance with her brother over the course of the next couple of weeks.

Despite these worries, nothing could dampen her spirits that afternoon, not after she had been able to see first-hand one of Akhenaten's famous boundary stelae. And so, an hour later, feeling happy but weary, covered in dust and desperately thirsty, Natasha clambered into the Jeep and sank back against the comfortable leather seat, grateful for the air conditioning which Mac, the driver, had ensured was switched on as soon as he saw them approaching. Even Nicky seemed to have run out of questions, and Kyle, after a quick glance across at the two of them, turned his attention to the scenery outside.

Chapter Six

Engrossed in polishing the handrail at the stern of the boat, Kyle's thoughts wandered back to that afternoon, to the way Natasha's eyes had widened in realisation when they stood before the boundary stela. He had paid extra for the attendant to open the smoked glass doors, knowing how interested she was in anything to do with Akhenaten. It had definitely been worth it to see the almost childlike excitement bubbling from her when she realised what they were looking at.

As he straightened to re-fold his polishing cloth, the soft pad of footsteps and faint traces of light perfume gave him a few seconds warning before Natasha appeared round the corner.

"Oh!" She seemed startled to see him. "Hi."

"Hi." When she didn't immediately respond, he assumed she was simply taking a stroll around the deck and, giving her a brief smile, returned to polishing the handrail.

Instead of continuing past him, she cleared her throat and, once again, he straightened and turned to face her. "I'm sorry, were you looking for me?"

She nodded, but didn't seem able to meet his eyes for more than a second at a time. She was nervous. "Yes, it was actually."

"Okay." He leaned against the newly polished railing to give her his full attention, but she remained silent until eventually he intervened. "Did you enjoy today?"

She blinked at the seemingly unexpected question. "I…yes, I did, thank you." She smiled up at him. "You were right. It was definitely worth it."

They fell into silence once more, and Kyle raised his eyebrows. "I'm sorry. I thought you wanted to speak to me."

She blushed, and rubbed at her cheek. "I know. I do, I'm sorry. I just…I'm not sure how to start."

He nodded slowly, his eyes narrowing as he observed her discomfort. He wondered what on earth she could have to say to him that would warrant making her so nervous. She had unpinned her hair, and it fell in loose waves over one shoulder and down the front of her pale-yellow sun dress. He resisted the urge to hook a finger under her chin and look into her eyes, to tell her that it didn't matter what she had to say to him; that it couldn't be that bad.

She took a deep breath. "Kyle. Nicky has really taken to you since we got here, and you've been so brilliant with him, spending so much time with him. He worships you."

He frowned and gave an uncertain smile. "It's not a problem. I think the world of Nicky, and I enjoy spending time with him."

When she refused to meet his gaze, and shifted uncomfortably, he felt a pang of apprehension. "Well, I didn't think there was a problem. Is there?"

"I just think it might be better if Nicky didn't spend so much time with you. I mean, I know it's usually Nicky who seeks you out but, if you could try not to encourage him, I think it would be better." Her words came out in a rush, and she nodded her head, swallowing nervously. "I would really appreciate it if you kept your distance."

"I…what?" Kyle stared at her in confusion. "Keep my distance?" He tried a smile, but it faded when she avoided his gaze. "I don't understand what you mean. Better for who?"

Confusion turned to disbelief; whatever he had imagined she was about to say, he had not expected to be told to back off his friendship with her brother. He felt as if he had been punched in the stomach. In the short time since they had met, he had formed a close bond with Nicky, and it suddenly dawned on him how much he had enjoyed being part of this family. And now, she was essentially saying his friendship wasn't wanted. A cold anger replaced his hurt and disappointment.

"Better for who? For Nicky…or you?" He kept his voice deliberately low but saw the quick, wary glance she threw at him.

"Well…Nicky, of course." She tried a smile that faded in the face of his anger. "Why would it be better for me?"

Kyle crumpled the polishing cloth into a tight ball and threw it to the ground. "I don't know. You tell me. Maybe you're jealous. Afraid that Nicky prefers my company to yours."

"No, no, of course not. That's not it at all."

"You bang on about wanting Nicky to have his independence, but when he does you don't like it, do you? You don't like to lose that control over him."

"No. You don't understand—"

"Oh, I understand, all right," he interrupted, his mouth twisting in disgust. "Tell me. Do you choose all Nicky's friends for him? I'd like to bet you do. And have you ever actually asked him if he wants to spend every weekend staying at your place, or is that something else you just decided suits you?"

Natasha didn't respond, but stared at him open-mouthed as he continued his harsh onslaught.

"My God, Lucy was only half right back on that first night, wasn't she? When she thought you were using Nicky as an excuse to not get involved with anyone." He gave a humourless laugh. "Yes, having him stay with you means you have the perfect excuse to avoid committing to a relationship, but more than that, it's about control, isn't it? It allows you to keep a tight grip on Nicky's life, and now you're scared you're losing that control."

He saw the colour drain from her face beneath her tan, and for a moment he regretted his words, knowing he had gone too far. But before he could speak, she came right back at him.

"All right, that's enough." She squared her shoulders and met his gaze at last, taking a step towards him, her eyes dark with what seemed like fury. "You have no understanding of what this means, do you? Of what it means to have Nicky see you as his new best friend. I asked you to try and distance yourself, because he won't understand why he won't ever see you again when we get back home. And that's a bigger deal than it sounds."

Kyle blinked. It had never occurred to him to think beyond the next few weeks, of what it would mean to Nicky, or indeed himself. He swallowed when she carried on.

"This is about my family; a family I have fought for since they tried to put Nicky into foster care, because they didn't think that, at eighteen years old, I could look after my fourteen-year-old brother when our parents died."

Natasha was physically shaking with anger, and he closed his eyes briefly before reaching out to her, but she stepped back out of his reach, her eyes glittering with unshed tears.

"Control?" She gave a bitter laugh. "You have no idea. Nicky stays with me every weekend because he wants to, because I want him to, and because we only have each other. It has nothing to do with my using him as an excuse for anything, not even as an excuse to avoid a relationship. Do you really think you can only ever go out on dates on a weekend? Heaven forbid someone would ask me to go and see a movie on a weekday."

She dashed a hand across her eyes and then looked up at him once more. His stomach gave a lurch at the coldness radiating from her gaze.

"But don't you worry about it, Kyle." She shook her head. "You do whatever you want. I'm sure you will anyway. And I'll pick up the pieces, just like I always do."

"Natasha, I—"

"You've stood in judgement of me since the day we met, and I've had enough. No wonder your wife left you, Kyle Richardson. You're an arrogant, sanctimonious bastard."

Kyle flinched as if he'd been struck, his hands curling around the railing behind him as her words bit deep and his knees threatened to buckle.

"I don't want anything more to do with you," she said coldly. "For the rest of this holiday you do your thing and I'll do mine. Stay away from me."

"Fine." It was all he could manage as she turned and walked away from him. He didn't move for a long time.

****

Natasha closed her cabin door and leaned against it, trying to control her breathing. She had never been so angry in all her life, but deeply regretted that dig about Kyle's wife. It was a low blow and had been uncalled for. She remembered the way he had recoiled at her words, pain flaring in his eyes, and she sank to the floor, pulling her knees up to her chest. Despite her fierce denials, his words pricked at her conscience.

What if he was right?

What if, subconsciously, she did try to exert too much control over Nicky's life? Yes, she constantly worried about him, worried that he would be taken advantage of, or would be hurt by other people's lack of understanding about his difficulties. But, despite her worries and fears, she had always tried to keep them to herself, to support his independence, hadn't she? Her gaze fell on the electronic tablet sitting on her bedside table, and she stared at it for a moment before scrambling to her feet and snatching it up. Minutes later she was hurrying along to the sun deck and, relieved to find it empty, switched on the tablet.

****

"Natasha! Wow, I didn't expect you to be video messaging me."

Natasha felt a lump form in her throat as she gazed at the image of her friend on the screen. She swallowed hard, telling herself to get a grip.

"Hi Sarah, I thought I'd check in, see if I've missed anything exciting?"

"Exciting? Here? Are you kidding?" Sarah laughed

and shook her head. "Come on, tell me what you've been up to. Is it really fantastic? Everything you dreamed of?"

Tears filled Natasha's eyes, and she found herself unable to speak. She pressed the back of her hand against her mouth, trying desperately to smile, and simply nodded her head.

Sarah's face fell and she leaned closer to the webcam, her eyes full of concern. "Oh Natasha, what's wrong? What's happened?"

"Nothing, nothing's wrong. I'm having a lovely time." She brushed the tears from her eyes and gave a bright smile. "I'm a bit emotional, that's all. No real reason."

Her friend frowned. "I don't believe you. Something's happened or you wouldn't be calling me."

To her complete dismay, Natasha burst into tears, sobbing desperately into her hands as she sat cross-legged on the deck.

"Oh, Tash, don't. Please don't." Sarah reached across to press her fingers against the screen. "Not when you're on the other side of the world and I can't do anything. Please don't cry. Tell me what's happened."

Struggling to regain her composure, Natasha sat up straight and wiped the tears from her face, taking long deep breaths while her friend waited patiently, her face a picture of concern. After a couple of minutes, she felt composed enough to speak.

"I'm sorry, I just…I don't really know where to start." She frowned at the screen. "Do you think I'm selfish and controlling?"

"What?" Sarah was taken aback. "What are you talking about? Of course, I don't."

"I mean about Nicky and…everything. Do you think

I try and control his life and…staying with me at weekends and things?"

"Natasha, I don't understand where this is coming from. Why are you asking me this?"

"It's Kyle," she said unhappily, picking at a loose thread on her dress. "And Lucy a bit, too."

"Lucy? Your aunt?" Sarah was becoming more confused by the minute. "And who is Kyle?"

Natasha sighed and shook her head. "Yes, Aunt Lucy. And Kyle is this guy, Aunt Lucy's friend. We're staying on his boat."

Sarah nodded and waited for her friend to continue.

"Lucy started it off. She had a bit to drink and suddenly started spouting off about how I use Nicky as an excuse not to get involved with anyone or do anything with my life. And then Kyle said I was jealous and wanted to control everything Nicky did, and that he only stays with me at weekends because it's what I want and not what he wants."

"And what do they know about anything?" Sarah said softly, her head on one side.

"But what if they're right?" Tears filled her eyes once again. "What if I am trying to control him without realizing it?"

"Tash. I've known you since primary school. I've seen everything you've done, everything you've had to fight for. The easy option would have been to let them put Nicky in foster care all those years ago." Sarah shrugged. "Nicky stays with you at weekends because that's what he loves to do, you know that."

"Well, I thought so too. He's never given me any reason to doubt it. But even if he did, it wouldn't matter." She lifted her hands in a helpless gesture. "He can do what he wants. It's not up to me, is it?"

"Exactly. This Kyle guy sounds like a right idiot. Don't listen to him, or to Lucy, for that matter."

When she didn't respond, Sarah once again leaned close to the screen. "Tash. You're not selfish and you're not controlling. You are the best sister Nicky could have. You've done so much for him and helped him become the lovely young man he is. You should be very proud of yourself. I know your mum and dad would be, too."

Unable to speak, she simply nodded and managed a watery smile.

"So, tell me. Apart from all this nonsense, have you managed to have a good time?"

This time, she managed a real smile. "Oh, Sarah, it's fantastic, it really is. It's everything I dreamed it would be. Despite the whole Nicky thing, Kyle has taken us to some amazing places."

"Good, I'm glad."

"Look, I'd better go, I need to do something with my face before dinner." She looked at her friend's smiling face on the screen. "Thank you, Sarah. I really needed that."

"Anytime, honey. You know that." Sarah blew her a kiss. "Just ignore them, and we'll catch up over a bottle of wine when you get back."

****

Standing on the walkway beneath the sun deck and staring blindly out across the Nile River, Kyle heard Natasha's footsteps running across the deck and down the stairs towards her cabin. He had not deliberately eavesdropped on her conversation, and had immediately started to leave when he realised she was calling her friend. But when she had started crying, he had been frozen to the spot, horrified to hear her sobs. He shook his head, wondering why he had said such awful things to her, things that were completely unfounded. But he knew why. He had wanted to hurt her as much as she had hurt him.

Although reluctant to explore the feelings Natasha aroused in him, scared of what he might find, he had no such difficulty in analysing his feelings for her brother. Nicky was full of fun and innocence and, having no relatives of his own, Kyle had unconsciously accepted Nicky's offer of friendship as he would a brother. He had been unprepared to have Natasha warn him off, and had lashed out at her in self-defence. Not that he could excuse his actions; what he had said was unforgivable.

Natasha's feistiness was one of the things that really drew him to her, and when she had given back as good as she had got, he had assumed the tears filling her eyes had been tears of anger. To hear her sobs of distress just now had been like a kick to the stomach, and he was reminded again of the times when she thought no-one was looking and he had glimpsed the vulnerability she tried to hide.

He dragged a hand through his hair. The irony of the situation was not lost on him. Having spent the last five years carefully avoiding getting too close to anyone, keeping a tight rein on his feelings for fear of losing someone else, here he was, lashing out at Natasha for telling him to do exactly that. *What was happening to him?*

****

Natasha walked into the salon looking as if she didn't give a damn about Kyle or his thoughts on how she lived her life. The long scarlet dress matched both her lipstick and the scarf tying her glossy hair into a ponytail high on top of her head. Kyle mentally urged her to meet his gaze as she walked across to the dining table, but she deliberately kept her eyes focused on her aunt and brother.

"Hello, Aunt Lucy." She smiled as she took the seat next to her aunt, sitting opposite Nicky. "What kind of a day have you had?"

"I've had a quiet day, thank you, Natasha. Nader has been keeping me company, though," said Lucy, blushing slightly before carrying on quickly. "And what about you, dear? Nicky has been telling me all about your day. We wondered where you were, actually. You disappeared as soon as you got back."

"Oh, I was desperate to freshen up; I was absolutely covered in dust," said Natasha easily. "And then I decided to catch up with Sarah, so I did a video call with her. We had a lovely day, though; seeing Akhenaten's boundary stela was amazing. I can't describe what that meant, what it felt like."

"I knew you'd enjoy that," said Lucy with a satisfied smile. "When Kyle told me where he was taking you, I knew you'd love it. I said that, didn't I, Kyle?"

"You did." He reached across to pour a glass of red for Lucy and white for Natasha, noting as he did so that, although she gave a polite nod of thanks, she managed to completely ignore him at the same time. In fact, she had not once acknowledged his presence since she had entered the room.

He studied her as she engaged in animated conversation with her brother and Lucy over dinner. She looked sexy as hell in that dress, and he longed to pull the scarf from her hair and run his fingers through the silken strands. He wondered at her composure this evening, having heard those broken, desperate sobs less than an hour ago. Her eyes were clear and bright, and she appeared relaxed and happy as she teased her brother when he complained he was missing his favourite television programme. She was a damn fine actress, and he was uneasy with her ability to hide her feelings behind that bright smile.

The rest of the evening was spent in the seating area of the salon, playing cards and some old board games which Nicky had found in one of the cupboards. Mahmoud and Nader joined them for the first time that evening, and their bemused reactions to Nicky's enthusiastic explanation of how to play Ludo were the cause of much laughter.

It was approaching midnight when Natasha turned down the opportunity to begin yet another game of cards and wished everyone a good night, wondering aloud how any of them had enough energy to continue. Her lips tightened when Kyle rose from his seat but, as she had all that evening, she ignored him and made her way to the door. She was halfway across the room when he said her name softly, and she continued without responding. The next moment he caught her arm, forcing her to a halt.

"Natasha, please. Can I talk to you?" His voice was low, obviously not wanting the others to hear their conversation.

For the first time that evening, she met his gaze, her eyes cold and unfriendly. "I meant what I said this afternoon; I have nothing to say to you, Kyle. And there is nothing you could say that is of any interest to me."

She deliberately looked down at his hand on her arm until he released her, and she quickly crossed to the door, closing it quietly behind her.

Feeling sick to the stomach, he returned to his seat to find Lucy observing him keenly. "Is everything all right?"

"Yes, everything's fine." He smiled, but it didn't quite reach his eyes and he could see Lucy was not convinced.

Chapter Seven

For the first time since their arrival in Egypt, the dawn brought with it a slight mist, although the sun shimmering behind the hazy veil left no doubt that, come midday, the heat would be intense. Kyle ran lightly up the steps to the sun deck, drawing in a quick breath when he reached the top and saw Natasha and Nicky were already there.

Dressed in long, white cotton trousers and a white vest top, Natasha was practising what he assumed was Tai Chi, while Nicky was sitting on the floor with his back against the railing, sketching in his book.

He stood for a moment, transfixed by her calm, graceful movements, and long deep breaths, exuding a sense of peace. She turned slowly, balancing on one leg with her arms stretched out in front. As she glanced up, her eyes met his gaze, and her calm, serene expression vanished, to be replaced with one of dislike and irritation. His heart sank. Walking towards her, he immediately stopped when she turned from him to pick up a towel.

"I'm sorry, I didn't mean to intrude." He held up his hand. "Please, carry on. I'll leave you to it."

"Forget it. The mood's gone," she snapped as she walked past him quickly. "Besides, it's your boat. You can go where you like."

Biting back his frustration, he made his way across

the deck to sit down next to Nicky, stretching his legs out in front of him. Nicky glanced up and grinned before returning to his drawing.

"Is she always so moody with people, or is it just me?" Kyle wondered aloud.

"It's just you." Nicky carefully smudged a line that was too defined for his liking before setting the sketchpad to one side and looking at Kyle, a broad smile creasing his handsome face. "I've never seen her in such a bad mood as often as I have this holiday."

"Great." He swept a hand wearily over his face. "Just great."

Nicky's expression grew serious, a frown creasing his forehead. "But I think maybe she's a bit fed up with me too. She asked me if I still wanted to come home every weekend."

"She did?" Kyle's heart skipped a beat, and his stomach tightened, cursing himself for ever raising the subject. He had spoken without thinking of the consequences, of the impact it might have upon both Nicky and Natasha.

"Do you think she doesn't want me to stay with her anymore?" Nicky suddenly looked very young, his green eyes worried. "She said she did, she said she liked me coming home, but…well, I don't know why she asked me then."

Kyle closed his eyes briefly. What a bloody mess. "It's my fault, Nicky. I know Natasha loves having you home with her, and I think she only asked you about it because of something I said to her."

"You?" Nicky looked confused. "What do you mean?"

Kyle sighed. "I sort of said that maybe you only

went home on a weekend because she told you to. I said you might prefer to stay at your flat." It sounded pathetic even to his own ears, and he grimaced.

"But I don't," said Nicky, looking more confused than ever. "I love coming home."

"I know…I…"

"Fridays are my favourite day," Nicky carried on, unaware of Kyle's growing discomfort with every word. "Because when I wake up on Friday, I know I'm going home after work. And Mondays are my worst day because that's the day I have to go back to my flat."

Kyle felt like weeping, but remained silent when Nicky looked at him earnestly. "But I go for tea with John on Mondays, because he knows they're my sad days so, you know, it's okay.

"I do like my flat, though," he continued, obviously not wanting Kyle to think he was being forced to stay somewhere he wasn't happy. "It's nice, and I know I have to be…independent." He said the word carefully, as though not fully understanding what it meant, only that it was something important. "My favourite thing would be to live with Tash all the time, but I know I can't and that it's right for me to have my flat. But I don't want to stop going home at the weekend."

"Look, don't worry about it, Nicky," said Kyle, shaking his head. "Like I said, I know Natasha loves having you, and she only asked you about it because of something I said. Just forget it. It's me being bloody stupid."

Nicky grinned. "You're not stupid. You're really clever, like that archaeologist from my favourite movie."

Leaning his head back against the rail, he looked at Nicky. "I don't feel particularly clever right now, I can tell you."

Nicky shrugged and picked up his sketchpad once more. "Cleverer than me."

Kyle watched the young man quickly become engrossed in his drawing, his pencil moving across the page with confidence. Spotting another sketchpad sitting on top of Nicky's bag, he reached for it. "Do you mind if I have a look?"

Nicky looked up and smiled, shaking his head. "No, go ahead. That's my first holiday one. I'm on my second already."

Kyle stared at him for a moment before beginning to flick through the pages. He quickly understood what Nicky meant. The first page was a sketch of a small, Victorian terraced house with a neat front garden, the front door standing ajar. Two suitcases sat on the doorstep. On the opposite page was a sketch of a taxi, with Natasha standing next to it and talking to the driver as he lifted the suitcases into the boot. Kyle shook his head, fascinated. These sketches were snapshots in time, almost like a photograph, and he was once again amazed with Nicky's talent as an artist, in his ability to capture scenes in such detail so quickly.

As he turned the pages of the pad, he realised that the sketchbook was a diary, recording the events of each day through sketches rather than words. One particular picture captured his attention. It was of a slightly overweight woman who, by the detail in the picture, was obviously a barista in one of the airport coffee lounges. The lines on her face spoke of weariness, but her eyes were kind, and she was smiling, her head on one side, and Kyle could imagine that she had been speaking to Nicky as he quickly sketched her portrait. It was stunning.

He flicked through the pages thoughtfully, his gaze taking in the hotel, the busy and winding streets of old Cairo, Natasha sitting drinking tea with an Egyptian shopkeeper, the pyramids at Giza, a beautiful one of his dahabeeyah, and a couple of himself. But his breath caught in his throat when he turned the page to find Natasha's eyes staring straight into his. It was a close-up sketch, and she was laughing, her hair caught up loosely in one of her scarves, tendrils curling around her face.

He gently traced her features with his fingers, wishing she would look at him with such happiness shining from her eyes.

"She's pretty, isn't she?"

Nicky's voice startled him, and he snatched his hand from the sketch. "She sure is."

He shut the sketchbook with a snap and got to his feet, causing Nicky to look up at him in surprise. "I need to apologise," he frowned. "Do you think she'll hear me out?"

"Oh yes." Nicky nodded positively. "Tash never stays angry for long."

Handing back his sketchbook, Kyle gave a wry smile. He didn't share Nicky's confidence.

****

Natasha was leaning against the same railing Kyle had been polishing yesterday, looking down into the Nile, captivated by the wake created as they slowly meandered down the river. Hearing footsteps, she glanced up and, with a sinking stomach, saw Kyle walking towards her. Why couldn't he leave her alone? She threw him a glance aimed at leaving him in no doubt that she had no wish to talk to him, before turning and walking away.

"Natasha, wait."

When she didn't respond, he strode after her, catching her elbow to turn her around to face him. "Hey, come on, please don't walk away from me." His tone was mild, conciliatory.

She snatched her arm from his grasp. "I told you last night, leave me alone."

When she turned from him, he caught her elbow once more, and she spun back, her eyes flashing angrily. "What is wrong with you?"

"I'm sorry." He frowned. "Okay? I'm sorry for what I said. It was stupid and I wasn't thinking. I didn't mean it."

"Then why say it?" She pulled her arm from his fingers once more, but remained where she was.

"I don't know," he said, with a helpless shrug.

Natasha's mouth twisted in disbelief. "Not good enough." She made as if to leave but his quiet voice stopped her.

"I was angry, and I lashed out," he admitted, turning to lean his forearms against the railing as he stared across the water towards the banks of the Nile. "What I said…it was wrong, and I didn't mean it. Any of it."

Against her will, Natasha felt her anger dissipating at his honesty, and she turned to rest her back against the railing next to him. Her weariness showed in her voice. "Have you any idea of the trouble you've caused?"

He dipped his head and gave a sigh. "Yes, I do. I spoke to Nicky this morning, and he told me about your conversation. I told him it was my fault, that I was an idiot."

"A bit of an understatement."

A reluctant smile caught his lips as he looked at her sideways. "Indeed. But I am truly sorry."

She responded with a half-smile, arms folded across her chest, her gaze fixed on the deck.

He pushed himself upright and moved to stand in front of her, hooking a finger under her chin when she refused to look him. "Truce?"

She didn't respond, concentrating on pretending that she wasn't affected at all by his nearness, and simply nodded, hugging her arms more tightly around herself as she attempted to ignore the temptation to run her hands over his chest. There must have been something in her face, something that gave her away because, when she lifted her gaze to his, he drew in a breath. She swallowed hard.

"You're on holiday. You should be enjoying yourself," he said softly, his gaze dropping to her mouth. "I can think of more enjoyable things for us to do than argue."

Cupping her face with his hands, he bent his head to kiss her, his lips moving against hers slowly and surely. Her resolved faltered, and the barrier created by her folded arms was broken as she allowed herself to slip her hands up over his chest to the back of his neck, her fingers slipping into his hair.

He closed the distance between them, pressing into her as she came up against the railing, and he groaned when she moved up onto tiptoes, her body sliding over his and causing him to react instantly. A wordless sound of need escaped his throat, and it sent a thrill spiking through her. She wrapped her arms around his shoulders to pull him closer, completely lost in his kiss.

This was what she wanted more than anything, she

realised in a sudden flash of clarity. The feelings he aroused in her, the way her body responded to his, were unlike anything she had ever experienced, and she kissed him back with a hunger that matched his own. When he pulled away from her slightly, she gave a soft moan of disappointment despite his lips never once leaving hers. But the distance between them was only momentary, as he lifted her up to sit on the railing before stepping close once more.

Neither of them heard the discreet cough from further along the walkway, and it was only after two further coughs, each getting louder in turn, that Kyle eventually heard someone calling his name.

"Kyle."

He jumped in surprise and turned his head, appearing somewhat dazed as he tried to focus on the man waiting patiently a little distance away, a broad grin creasing his face.

"I am sorry for interrupting you." He didn't look in the least bit sorry.

"Nader." Kyle cleared his throat, and belatedly realised that his hands were still firmly placed over Natasha's rather shapely rear where she perched on the railing. He snatched his hands away, stepping back from her embrace and running a hand distractedly through his hair. "No problem. Er…is there a problem? What did you want?"

"No problem," Nader smiled, his liquid brown eyes showing obvious amusement at his friend's discomposure. "We will be mooring up shortly."

"Of course, of course." Kyle nodded to Nader. "Right, I'm on my way."

****

Natasha couldn't help but smile as she slipped from the railing, and turned to hurry along the walkway on unsteady legs, pressing her hands to her cheeks in an effort to reduce the burning feeling.

How embarrassing to be caught making out like a teenager.

She closed her eyes in mortification, but then started to giggle. Oh, but it had been wonderful, and so amusing to see Kyle's obvious discomfort at being caught unawares. Running lightly up the stairs to the sundeck, she observed Lucy sitting in one of the rattan chairs under the canopy, staring off into space.

As she took her seat, Lucy glanced across to smile at her niece before returning her gaze to the shore, but quickly did a double take, sitting up straight to look more closely at Natasha.

"Well, my dear, forgive my bluntness, but I have to say that you look as if you have been well and truly kissed!" She stared in surprise, her gaze travelling from the kiss-swollen lips and slightly reddened skin around Natasha's mouth that gave away her recent close contact with stubble, to the slightly lopsided ponytail that was threatening to break free from her habitual scarf.

Natasha could feel the colour rising along her throat when Lucy smiled in satisfaction, sitting back in her chair and nodding knowingly.

"I knew it. Good for you."

"Do you think?" Natasha was almost relieved to be able to talk to someone about her confused feelings, although slightly uncomfortable that that someone was her aunt.

"Of course I think," Lucy responded immediately. "You deserve a bit of fun. Kyle's a lovely man, and who can blame you or him for having a holiday fling?"

"But what about his girlfriend? What about Gemma?"

"What about her?" Lucy dismissed that suggestion with a wave of her hand. "She's not here, is she? And I've only your word to say that she is actually his girlfriend."

"Aunt Lucy…" Natasha wasn't quite sure what to say, surprised that her aunt was so open-minded.

Lucy seemed to read her mind, and her expression softened. "I'm not such an old fuddy-duddy, Natasha dear. Life is too short. A bit of fun never hurt anyone, as long as you both know what you're signing up for."

Natasha stared at her thoughtfully. A bit of fun. Was that what she wanted? Would she be happy with that, or did she want more? She knew she wanted Kyle, wanted to feel the feelings he aroused in her, but was that enough? She mentally shook her head; no, she wanted more. She wanted Kyle's heart and soul, and that was the problem.

Before she could explore those thoughts any further, Lucy's soft voice broke into her thoughts.

"Natasha. I've been trying to think about how best to say something to you, how to broach a difficult subject, somewhat related to what we've just been discussing."

"You and Nader?" said Natasha gently.

Lucy gasped in surprise. "You know?"

Natasha nodded with a smile. "Kyle noticed first."

Tears filled her aunt's eyes, and she reached for the handkerchief tucked securely in her bra strap. "Oh Tash, are you very angry with me? I've been so lonely without my Joe, and Nader is such good company. He knew Joe, too."

"Aunt Lucy, of course I'm not angry with you." Natasha reached across to hold Lucy's hand. "Why would I be? I know how much you loved Uncle Joe, but he's been gone for two years now, and you are entitled to have some fun yourself. That's what he would have wanted, I know it."

Lucy gave a few rapid blinks, her relief palpable, and leaned forward to hug Natasha to her. "Thank you. You have no idea how much that means to me."

She settled back into her seat, blew her nose, and nodded firmly to herself. "Well. So that's settled then. We'll both have a bit of fun, a bit of romance in Egypt, and why not?"

Heaving a rather shaky sigh, Lucy turned once more to watch the banks of the Nile drift lazily by, and Natasha leaned back into her seat, closing her eyes. She wasn't sure she felt as optimistic about the prospect of a holiday romance. As tempting as it was — and it was tempting — it would surely be less painful in the long run if she and Kyle kept things strictly platonic. To pretend she would be happy with a casual fling would simply be fooling herself. No, she would be best keeping Kyle at arm's length in future.

The decision made, she gave a resigned sigh, reaching into her trouser pocket for her phone, choosing her favourite playlist, and pushing the earplugs firmly into her ears in an attempt to drown out the irritating voice in the back of her head telling her she was a fool and a coward.

****

Natasha started in surprise at the gentle tap on her wrist. Opening her eyes, she saw her aunt smiling down at her.

"We're here, dear. Are you ready to go?"

She must have dozed off, and rubbed her face in an effort to wake up. "Oh right, yes. Just let me get my things."

Five minutes later, after a quick dash to her cabin, she ran lightly down the gangplank, pulling her bag over her shoulder and slipping on her sunglasses and hat, hurrying to where the others were waiting for her. She was surprised to see Lucy with them, and fell into step beside her as they made their way along the bankside to a rather ugly and modern single storey brick building that proved to be the ticket office.

"I didn't realise you were coming today, Aunt Lucy?"

"Well, although Joe and I regularly visited many of the sites along the Nile, I've only been to Amarna once before, and I thought I would like to see it again."

A tingle of excitement ran along Natasha's spine as she slipped her arm through her aunt's. "I can't wait to see it. I hope I won't be disappointed – it's the one place I've always wanted to visit."

Kyle and Nicky went into the ticket office, leaving the two women waiting outside in the shade, but they soon reappeared and led them to the large and equally ugly gateway which marked the entrance to the site.

Natasha tried not to be too critical, but as first impressions went, the maroon painted entrance — a crude attempt at a mock-temple pylon gate— did not instil her with confidence. Once through the entrance, a tarmac track led off towards cliffs that could be seen in the distance, and Natasha automatically looked for the Jeep that Kyle always arranged for them. Today, however, there was no vehicle in sight, and she wondered if the tombs and ancient city were within walking distance. The heat was intense, sweat already trickling along her spine, and she hoped it was not too long a walk.

To her surprise, instead of walking down the track, Kyle turned off to the side, flicking her a grin and a wink. "I'm glad to see you're dressed appropriately."

She glanced down at her cream linen trousers and flat pumps in confusion, wondering what he meant, before looking up and gasping in surprise when she saw him talking to a young Egyptian standing beside four camels crouched in the shade of a rather limp-looking palm tree.

"Oh, please tell me you're not joking." Her face lit up and she ran over to Kyle. "Are we really going to ride on camels?"

"We certainly are." He took in her obvious delight with a smile. "I wasn't sure if it would be your sort of thing, but I thought it was an experience you shouldn't miss out on."

"Oh no, I'd love to try it."

"Phew. They stink." Nicky joined them, waving his hand in front of his nose, and glancing rather warily at the large animals, who calmly returned his gaze.

Natasha slowly walked up to the camels. She had to admit the pungent smell was a little overpowering, but she was nevertheless captivated by the languid-looking beasts, with their long eyelashes and docile brown eyes.

"This one. I'll ride this one." She pointed to the off-white camel who grunted softly when she approached.

Kyle spoke in rapid dialect to the Egyptian, allocating camels to Lucy then Nicky, who still appeared a little unsure about this mode of transport.

"Come on, Nicky. This is an adventure. They rode camels in your film, didn't they?"

Nicky pulled a face, but allowed Lucy to nudge him towards his camel. "I suppose so."

"Oh, it's been a while since I last rode a camel, but I'm sure it's like riding a bike; you never forget." To Natasha's amazement, Lucy deftly swung herself up into the saddle of her camel, gave a flick of the reins, and expertly balanced herself as the camel lurched to its feet. Lucy turned around to gaze at them expectantly, a rather smug expression on her face.

"See, nothing to it. Come on, let's get going."

Natasha couldn't help but admire her aunt's spirit, and turned back to her own camel, laughing softly. "Right then. As the lady says, let's get going."

The young Egyptian hovered close, pointing out the single stirrup resting against the camel's flank, and motioned for Natasha to hold onto the saddle's wooden handle. With more confidence than she felt, she stepped into the stirrup, grabbed hold of the saddle, and swung her left leg over the camel's back. With the Egyptian watching her critically, she shuffled herself until she was sitting in the middle of the saddle, and holding onto the handles at the front and back.

Obviously happy with her seated position, he gently touched his stick to the camel's hind quarters and rapped out a short command. Immediately the camel started to get to its feet, straightening up from the back legs first, and Natasha automatically leaned back to prevent herself from tumbling over the camel's neck, and then forwards as it straightened up its front legs.

Feeling inordinately pleased with herself for

negotiating this tricky exercise without falling off, she glanced across to where Kyle was assisting Nicky. She watched with a smile as her brother scrambled onto the camel with a rather doubtful expression. There was one rather dodgy moment when it looked as if Nicky might slide off, but Kyle managed to shove him back before he reached the point of no return. When he was satisfied that everyone was safely installed on their respective camels, Kyle turned to mount his own.

They set off in single file along the tarmac road, and Natasha gripped the saddle handles hard, her heart thumping painfully in her chest, but soon became used to the gentle swaying gait of her camel. She saw Kyle in front of her, one long leg curled around the handle of his saddle and looking as if he rode this mode of transport every day of his life. After a further five minutes of debate with herself, she took a deep breath and slowly lifted her left leg, inching it over the camel's neck to wrap it around her saddle. There was one heart-stopping moment when she felt herself slipping, but managed to grip the handle and right herself before completing the manoeuvre. A little more shuffling and she found that the side-saddle position Kyle had assumed was indeed much more comfortable; she began to relax, allowing her body to sway in time with the camel.

Glancing over her shoulder, she could see Nicky now looking completely at ease and chattering nonstop to Lucy behind him and, from what she could make out, indicating that he really liked camels despite the smell. Facing forwards once more, she saw Kyle slowing his camel just enough to allow her to draw alongside him.

"Enjoying it?" he asked.

"Oh yes. Colin and I are doing well, thank you."

"Colin?"

"Yes. That's what I've called my camel. He's lovely."

His grin sent her heart rate soaring, and she smiled back before gesturing towards the cliffs. "Is that where we're going?"

"No, we're going to turn off in a little while and make our way to the ancient city. Once we've had a look around, I've arranged for the Jeep to pick us up and take us around the tombs over in the north, and then the Royal Tombs further out. The site is spread out across a fairly substantial area, so it's not really practical to cover it all on camel, I'm afraid."

As he moved out in front of her once again, Natasha couldn't help but smile with happiness. This was the Egypt she had dreamed about: camels, sand, dust, searing heat, and an ancient city. Once again, she marvelled at the lack of tourist activity and, although she guessed many of the locals must rely on tourism for their livelihood, she was secretly pleased that it meant she could enjoy exploring it all in almost perfect isolation.

****

They reached the outskirts of the ancient city of Akhetaten half an hour later. Once a magnificent sprawling metropolis, it was now reduced to mounds of sand and debris, and Kyle steered his camel off the tarmac road where he expertly dismounted. Instinctively, the other camels followed suit, all of them dropping to their knees, front first, to settle down quite happily in the sand. This caused a number of gasps and cries of surprise from both Natasha and Nicky, unprepared as they were for such a speedy dismount.

Natasha realised Colin was going to crouch down

just as he bent his front legs and, with a muffled shriek, managed to lean back in time. Nicky was not so fortunate. He was too busy turning around to talk to Lucy to realise what was happening, and he tumbled straight over his camel's neck to land in a dishevelled heap on the hot sand. His camel grunted and sniffed curiously at Nicky's jacket, no doubt hoping to find a piece of carrot or some other tasty morsel of food.

"You okay, Nicky?" Natasha called across to her brother when he remained motionless for a couple of seconds before sitting up and shaking his head vigorously. Kyle was beside him quickly, and crouched down in front of him.

"Nicky?"

Nicky looked up with a broad grin on his face. "Wow. That was exciting."

Kyle returned his smile, helping him to his feet. "You sure you're okay? Are you hurt anywhere?"

Nicky shrugged his shoulders experimentally, shook his arms and legs out, and jumped up and down. "Nope. Nothing hurts."

"Good."

Kyle ruffled the younger man's hair, handed him back the baseball cap lying on the sand beside him, and looked up as Natasha approached. He gave her a reassuring nod, running a gentle hand along her arm as he turned away and squinted back up the road along which they had come.

"Mac should be coming with the Jeep any minute…ah, there he is."

The Jeep came into sight and, moments later, pulled up alongside them. Mac gave them all a wave, but remained in the car, while the other occupant alighted.

Natasha immediately recognized the young Egyptian owner of the camels, and he gave them a wide grin as he hurried over to his livestock to meet Kyle.

Wandering a little way down the road by herself, Natasha was suddenly struck by the oddest sensation that she had been here before. It wasn't déjà vu in the strictest sense, because she could easily imagine the city as it had been in Akhenaten's time. Instead of the low, crumbling brick walls, she could see the towering walls of pristine buildings standing on either side of the road on which she stood.

Gasping in amazement, she could even see people going about their everyday business, her ears suddenly ringing with the sounds of people chattering, laughing, and shouting, amidst other strange noises she couldn't identify. Her senses were assaulted, and she was overpowered by the smell of animal dung, unwashed bodies, food smells, and the musky scent of incense.

A voice close to her ear suddenly penetrated her stupor, and she turned her head to see Kyle looking at her with a puzzled expression. She blinked in confusion, turning back to the busy scene in front of her but it had gone, vanishing as quickly as it had appeared.

"Natasha?" His hand on her elbow pulled her around to face him. "Are you okay?"

"I…yes, yes, I'm fine." She rubbed her cheek thoughtfully. "That was weird."

"What was?"

Unable to help herself, she looked back at the ancient city but was unable to repeat the vision, and she shook her head with a frown. "Doesn't matter. You wouldn't believe me anyway."

She started to walk away from him but his hand on

her arm stopped her. "Try me."

She gave him a long, considered glance, one which he returned steadily. "Okay. I just had a…a bit of a weird déjà vu type of thing."

She took his quick nod to be a sign to continue, and pointed behind her with a thumb. "I was looking down the road at the old ruins and, suddenly, it was as if I was there…back when it was all new. I could see and hear people…everything. It was amazing. And I can't explain it."

She looked at him uncertainly, trying to gauge his reaction. When he remained silent, she dropped her gaze and shrugged her shoulders. "Too much sun, no doubt."

After a moment Kyle hooked a finger under her chin to raise her eyes to his. "Maybe." He gave her a slow smile. "Or maybe that site attendant at Tuna el-Gebel was right, maybe *The Beautiful One Has Come* does walk the earth once more, after all."

"Nefertiti?" She looked at him in confusion. "What, like I'm some kind of reincarnation? Is that what he meant?"

"Why not? You're certainly the dead spit of her."

"You're joking." She gave him a half-hearted push, not sure if he was making fun of her. "And I'm sure you don't believe in all that kind of stuff."

"How do you know what I believe?" He tipped his head on one side. "How else would you explain what you saw?"

"I don't know. A good imagination? I've read so much about ancient Egypt, seen artists' impressions, that kind of thing. What if I was projecting all that information into a vision? I don't know how else I could explain it."

"It's possible, I suppose." Kyle shrugged. "Reincarnation, inherited memories; people believe all sorts of stuff."

"What about you? Do you believe in reincarnation?"

"I don't know, to be honest. A lot of intelligent people believe in it, a lot don't. I don't have an opinion either way, really." He gave a sudden smile. "Hey, it sounds like it was an amazing scene you experienced, whatever it was. Don't knock it."

His smile was infectious, giving her butterflies in the pit of her stomach and causing her to relive those wonderful moments in his arms when his searing kisses had left her breathless. He might have been sharing those same thoughts, because he moved a step closer, his eyes dropping to her mouth, but Nicky's voice effectively ended the moment.

"It's flipping hot here, you two. Why are we just standing around?"

Unsure whether she was disappointed or relieved, Natasha adjusted her hat as Kyle stepped away from her, laughing at Nicky's impatience.

"All right, come on, let's get going. Nicky's right, it's too hot to stand in the sun all day."

A quick glance up the road showed Natasha that the young Egyptian was already well on his way to the entrance, his camels following him in single file as his voice floated back on the air, singing either to himself or his camels — or perhaps both.

With Kyle and Natasha walking out in front, Nicky and Lucy followed behind as they explored the site. Initially they followed the tarmac road that continued straight through the city, then took the original course of the old Royal Road, which effectively split Akhetaten in two. Natasha knew that, unlike other ancient cities, much of Akhetaten had been built using mud bricks instead of the huge stone blocks usually used, and this had enabled the city to be built more quickly. But it had also meant, following Akhenaten's reign, that the city had been much easier to disassemble.

They wandered leisurely towards the original Great Aten Temple, which unlike traditional temples, had no roof, enabling worshippers to bask in the glory of the sun god Aten. From there, they moved to the site of the Foreign Office archives, where the Amarna letters had been discovered. Natasha could well understand Kyle's initial reluctance to bring them to Amarna. He was right, the city had been most effectively razed to the ground, leaving very little to see, and it was difficult to distinguish where the original walls would have stood. But Natasha didn't care; it was everything she had expected and more.

When Kyle led them across to where the main royal residence had once stood, she had no difficulty in imagining how impressive it must have been, but this time it was simple imagination and not the same surreal experience as before. They came to a momentary halt as Kyle explained how the royal palace and state palace had stood facing each other on opposite sides of the road, with the *window of appearances* spanning the road and linking the two buildings, similar to a covered bridge. His enthusiastic explanation was peppered with regular, gentle touches to her hand, arm or shoulder, as if to emphasise a point. And, despite her previous determination to keep her distance, she fell deeper under his spell.

****

It had been a wonderful day; the fulfilment of a lifetime's ambition almost. Back on board the dahabeeyah and in need of some quiet reflection, Natasha went straight to her cabin. She sank onto the window seat, staring through the window while she mentally retraced their steps. Despite Kyle's concern that she would find the desolate, ruined city a disappointment, she had instead been captivated. The tombs, although claustrophobic and something of a hike from the city itself, retained a solemn, mystical aura despite their state of disrepair.

Nicky had also appeared to sense something different about this site. Perhaps it had something to do with the almost desperate hatred that had rained down on Akhenaten's beloved city all those thousands of years ago, causing it to be destroyed and abandoned after his death. Perhaps Kyle was right about inherited memories, or maybe some of the despair and sadness still clung to the few crumbling bricks that remained. Whatever it was, Nicky had been inspired by the ancient city, his pencil flying across the page to capture the poignancy of the scene.

Reaching into her shoulder bag, Natasha fished out her mobile phone and flicked through the photographs she had taken that day. While not truly reflecting the atmosphere of the city, she was nevertheless pleased with the shots she had taken, and gave a soft chuckle as she scrolled through to see a close-up of Colin gazing serenely at her as she took his photograph. With a satisfied smile, she dropped her phone onto the bed and pulled the blinds closed across the window before undressing and stepping into the shower.

****

Wandering into the salon half an hour later, Natasha was greeted by Kyle and Nicky obviously sharing a joke at her aunt's expense.

"Tash, Tash. Guess what. Aunty Lucy's got a mobile phone." Nicky looked at her expectantly, as if he had told a funny joke.

"I know she has." She looked at him with a puzzled smile.

"But she never has it switched on." He grinned, squeezing his hands into fists by his side as he physically tried to contain his excitement in order to provide a moment of anticipation before he came out with the punchline. "And her friends have to send her letters because she never gets their texts!"

"I have my phone in case I need it in an emergency," said Lucy, somewhat defensively, looking beseechingly at Natasha for support. "And there is nothing wrong in preferring the old-fashioned art of letter writing."

"Of course, there isn't," Natasha agreed, with a smile and a secret wink to Nicky. "Letter writing is becoming something of a lost art. How did these two Philistines learn your secret, anyway?"

"Oh, of course, you weren't here." Relieved to be able to change the subject, Lucy reached out to pick up an envelope from the coffee table, flicking Natasha a quick glance as she did so. "Sit down, dear, you look as if you're not intending to stay."

About to take the empty armchair, Natasha was caught off balance when Kyle's hand closed around her wrist and pulled her towards him, resulting in her sitting down rather heavily by his side on the sofa. Blushing slightly, she glanced across at him and was rewarded by a satisfied grin as he settled back, one arm casually resting along the back of the sofa behind her.

"It's from Netta." Lucy wafted the letter in front of her. "She heard I was on the Nile, and sent one of her men out to deliver an invitation to a party she's holding tomorrow night."

Somewhat distracted by the delicious sensations caused by Kyle's fingertips lazily tracing swirls over her shoulder, Natasha tried to concentrate on what her aunt was saying. "She sent someone out along the Nile with an invitation? But we could have been miles away. It was a bit lucky he found us, wasn't it?"

"Oh no, dear. News travels fast on the grapevine here. Kyle and I are well known up and down the Nile, and Netta will have had her spies out as soon as she arrived back in Egypt. Nothing gets past Netta." A slight pinkish flush touched Lucy's cheeks, perhaps as she realised there might be more for her friend to know than she would have liked.

"And she's invited you to a party?" Natasha prompted, aware of her sudden discomfort. "Where is it?"

"Oh, not just me, dear. She's invited all of us." Lucy smiled gratefully at her niece. "And she's on the Nile, too; has her own boat. Nothing as nice as this one, of course, Kyle. She's only a day's cruise ahead of us, so it shouldn't interfere with our itinerary. It's all worked out perfectly."

"It's a fancy-dress party as well, Tash. How cool is that?" Nicky grinned.

Kyle groaned by her side and dropped his head back on the sofa, raising his gaze to the ceiling. "Fancy dress? You forgot to mention that a few minutes ago, Lucy."

"Did I?" She looked across at him with an innocent

expression.

"Yes. You did." He lifted his head to give her a knowing smile. "Perhaps you three should go. I'll stay and keep an eye on the boat."

"Absolutely not." Lucy favoured him with a frown. "The invitation was for everyone; Nader and Mahmoud included. It would be rude and churlish not to go."

"Oh, come on, Kyle, pleeeaaase." Nicky gave a dramatic sigh. "Oh, please go, it'll be cool."

Kyle turned to Natasha, his fingers now softly caressing the nape of her neck. "What about you, Natasha? What do you think about a fancy-dress party?"

Swallowing against the sudden dryness at the back of her throat, she was unable to look away from his intense gaze. "I…um…I think it might be fun. Something different."

There was a long pause as he held her gaze. "Okay. Count me in," he said softly, before looking across to Lucy. "Leave the costumes to me. I know where I can get hold of everything we need."

"Oh, now I don't know about that," the older woman said doubtfully. "I don't want you dressing me up in something embarrassing because I'm insisting you go."

"Trust me," he said with a grin.

Chapter Eight

Casting a final glance in the mirror, Kyle readjusted his waistcoat, secured the pocket watch, and shrugged on his tweed jacket, musing as he did so that Natasha had somehow managed to remain elusive today; friendly and responsive to his flirtatious behaviour, but nonetheless elusive.

They had spent the entire day sailing along the Nile, but he had found little opportunity to spend time alone with her, always finding her with Lucy or Nicky, or escaping the heat of the day in her cabin. Mahmoud and Mac had sped off in the Jeep first thing this morning with a list of various items of clothing, along with the places where Mahmoud could expect to beg, borrow, or buy them. He hoped this god-awful fancy dress party tonight would allow him the opportunity to spend some time with Natasha; he'd missed her today.

The salon was empty when he walked in, and he poured himself a whisky, leaning against the bar and attempting to ignore the unusual sensation fluttering in the pit of his stomach. He wasn't sure if he was nervous about the party or about seeing Natasha in the costume he had arranged for her. Or, indeed, if he was just desperate to see her again. Ridiculous.

He glanced up as the door burst open, and grinned when Nicky came in at speed. The worn leather jacket, tan coloured slacks, and whip coiled on his hip, made him every inch the archaeological hero.

"Look at me!" Nicky whirled in excitement before pulling on the brand-new fedora, and coming to a halt in front of Kyle. "This is brilliant. I can't wait for the party."

"You look just like him, Nicky." Kyle slapped him on the back, his nerves receding a little as he enjoyed the younger man's excitement. "How long do you reckon we'll have to wait for the girls?"

Nicky groaned. "Oh, I hope they're not ages. I want to go to the party."

With that, the door opened again, and Kyle caught his breath when Lucy entered the room, followed by Natasha, looking more than a little self-conscious. The white chiffon column dress fell in soft folds to the floor, and her hair was caught up under the Nefertiti-style sapphire crown, leaving her neck and shoulders bare. She was achingly beautiful, and for a moment he was unable to move, breathe, or do anything except concentrate on remaining upright.

"Oh Kyle, you wonderful, wonderful man." Lucy's voice brought him out of his stupor, and he dragged his gaze from Natasha to her aunt just in time to catch her when she flung herself into his arms. "You remembered."

He held Lucy tightly as she gave a muffled sob. "I wasn't sure if you'd like it or if it would upset you."

She pulled back slightly from his embrace to place her hand on his cheek. "It's perfect and quite wonderful, thank you."

"You look really pretty, Aunty Lucy." Nicky smiled and nodded. "I like your dress."

The twenties-style dress suited her. The drop waist

and longer, fringed hemline had a slimming effect, while the muted emerald beads overlaying the dark green fabric of the dress complimented Lucy's tanned skin.

Planting a kiss on Kyle's cheek, she turned to Nicky with a wistful smile. "I was wearing a dress very similar to this one when I first met your Uncle Joe. That was at one of Nessa's fancy-dress parties, too. I have a photograph of that party on my sideboard at home, and Kyle is a very special man to have remembered that. It's called a flapper dress."

Nicky frowned. "A flapper dress? What's flappy about it?"

While Lucy laughingly tried to explain to Nicky about the dress, Kyle moved across to where Natasha was standing watching with an amused smile. She turned to him as he approached.

"You are beautiful," he said softly, gently lifting her chin with his finger and gazing into her eyes, emphasized this evening by a soft line of kohl. "Nice eye make-up."

Again, that hint of colour spreading across her delicate cheekbones. "I found a picture of Nefertiti and tried to copy the eyeliner." She shrugged. "Do you think I look all right? It's not too much?"

"Stunning. You take my breath away."

He was rewarded with a smile and a brief kiss that was over far too quickly when she stepped back to regard him critically. He turned full circle, arms outstretched before raising a quizzical eyebrow. "So, what do you think?"

His hair was slicked back from his forehead, and the false moustache hopefully looked realistic. The old-fashioned tweed suit, with the rather baggy trousers, didn't look as bad as he had expected and were actually very comfortable. But he was unable to read anything from her expression as she stood with her head on one side, her critical gaze taking in his appearance from head to toe. His body tingled in response to her light gaze, and his breath quickened at the unexpected sensuality of the moment.

"Howard Carter, I presume," she said at last, a smile curving her lips. "Though I didn't realise Mr. Carter was so very handsome."

He blinked in surprise, his heart leaping in his chest as he stared at her. Her eyes widened, colour flooding her cheeks, and she turned away before he could respond.

"What time do we need to be at the party? Should we be going? I think we should be going, don't you? What about Nader and Mahmoud? Are they ready, do you think?" Her voice was a little higher than normal.

"Yes, yes." Lucy tucked her arm through Nicky's. "You're right, we should be on our way. Nader and Mahmoud have decided to spend some time with relatives who live close by, and have already left. Now, has everybody got everything they need?"

"Almost." Kyle strode across the room and reached behind the bar to retrieve a flat, square box. He returned to stand in front of Natasha, and held the box out to her. "The final piece of your costume."

Carefully lifting the lid, she gasped at the broad collar necklace nestled inside. Multi-faceted glass beads of varying shapes and sizes in blues, greens and reds, were held together in rows by bands of gold-coloured metal.

"Oh, Kyle, it's beautiful."

He lifted the necklace from the box and turned her

around. "Here, let me. Now don't get excited, they're only glass beads. I don't want you thinking I've spent thousands on rubies, sapphires and emeralds." He smiled when she faced him once more. "You may be the living reincarnation of one of Egypt's most famous queens, but I'm afraid you'll have to make do with a replica."

The lightness of his words was belied by the intensity of his blue gaze, and once again he was aware of the chemistry crackling between them. She held his gaze for a moment longer before swallowing and acknowledging his playful remarks with a wry smile, before turning to the others. "So, how do I look?"

"Like a queen, my dear."

"Just like Queen Nefertiti, Tash. It's awesome."

"Oh, wait." Lucy suddenly started rummaging in her beaded clutch bag. "We need a photograph. Quick, Tash, you stand there; Kyle, you next to her; and Nicky here, on the other side."

She set the camera up on the bar and hurried back to stand next to Nicky, smiling brightly towards the camera. "Any minute now."

Kyle pulled Natasha into his side, his hand on her waist, and she lifted her head to glance up at him just as the shutter went off, earning a sigh and an eye-roll from Lucy when she reviewed the photograph on the camera's digital screen.

"Oh, Tash, you weren't looking."

"May I?" Kyle took the camera from her and peered at the digital image. Lucy and Nicky were smiling into the viewfinder and, although he and Natasha were looking at each other rather than the camera, it was a captivating photograph. The costumes and the period backdrop of the dahabeeyah salon lent an air of romance to the vignette, more so because of the tender glances between the two of them.

"I'd like a copy of that photograph, Lucy," he said casually, handing the camera back and ushering everyone towards the door.

****

They had moored directly behind Netta's boat and, as they boarded, Natasha reflected once again how lucky they were to be spending their holiday cruising the Nile in the *Aten's Dream*. While beautiful, immaculate, and fitted with every modern convenience, Netta's much larger boat lacked the romance and warmth of Kyle's period dahabeeyah.

The party was already in full swing when they arrived, and she was relieved to see the vast majority of guests in fancy dress. Unsurprisingly, there was a strong Egyptian theme with a range of pharaoh, Cleopatra, and Nefertiti costumes, but there were also a few oddities, including a rather overweight lycra clad superhero, who looked uncomfortably hot in the skin-tight costume; one very dashing archetypal secret agent; and a rather gruesome-looking zombie. Netta herself made a striking Cleopatra, complete with a heavy black wig and thick eyeliner. She flung her arms around Lucy when they arrived, her eyes sparkling with sudden tears as she took in her friend's outfit.

"Lucy, darling, you look beautiful. Just as you did all those years ago when Joe begged me to introduce you to him."

Lucy nodded, suddenly unable to speak, and retrieved a tissue from her purse to dab at her eyes. Netta cleared her throat briskly. "Kyle, darling, you get more handsome every time I see you; you look marvellous.

And you must be Natasha and Nicky. My, my, what a beautiful family you all make."

The next few minutes passed in a whirl of introductions to other guests, before Netta spied someone across the room and grasped Lucy's arm purposefully. "Now, Lucy, here is someone you have to meet…"

As the two women made their way across the room, Nicky disappeared in the direction of the buffet table, announcing he was hungry. Natasha watched as he piled food onto his plate and struck up a conversation with the dashing secret agent as easily as if they'd known each other for years.

"Okay." She gazed around the room somewhat apprehensively. She didn't find it as easy to mingle with strangers as her brother did. Looking up at Kyle, her stomach did a little flip when she realised he was watching her intently. "So, I suppose you know a lot of people here?"

He gave a soft chuckle and shook his head. "Difficult to tell really, with all these costumes."

She nodded, her eyes drifting back to where her brother had now joined a small crowd of people and was talking animatedly, his hand automatically straying into his hero archaeologist-style shoulder bag to pull out his sketchbook.

"Are you hungry? Do want something to eat, or can I get you a drink?" Kyle's hand on her elbow brought her gaze back to his, but before she could answer, they were interrupted by a large bear of a man dressed as Julius Caesar, and who enveloped Kyle in a hug.

"Kyle, my friend, I had no idea you would be here." His booming voice caused a number of people to turn in their direction, but he carried on unperturbed. "Did Netta fail to inform you it was fancy dress?" He gave a large belly laugh, slapping Kyle on the back before turning his ample frame towards Natasha. "And who is this fine young woman?"

"Natasha, this is Professor Simon Corkish, one of our most renowned lecturers in Egyptology, believe it or not. And he also happens to be one of my oldest friends." He grinned when Simon pretended to preen at the compliment. "Simon, meet Natasha Morgan. She's Lucy's niece and is here on holiday with her brother, Nicky. They're staying with me on the boat."

"Are they now?" Simon raised an eyebrow towards his friend and put his arm around Natasha's shoulder, leaning in close to stage-whisper in her ear. "Well, my dear, I think we need to have something of a chat about that."

She spent the next hour or so listening to Simon and Kyle trying to outdo each other with tall tales of the various escapades they had shared. Simon had a tendency to embellish his stories, or at least she hoped they were embellished, but she enjoyed his company very much, and couldn't remember the last time she had laughed so much. She also enjoyed seeing Kyle so relaxed and happy, his sense of humour coming through strongly as he gave his friend as good as he got.

Simon eventually paused for breath, mopping his sweating brow with a rather crumpled looking handkerchief, and gazing around the room. Heaving a dramatic sigh, he laid a heavy hand on Kyle's shoulder. "Well, my friend, it looks as if our fun is over. We've obviously been making far too much noise. I have been summoned."

Natasha followed Simon's gaze to where Netta was beckoning him furiously, and mouthing what looked like "You need to meet him", pointing to the rather short pharaoh standing beside her.

"Natasha, my dear, it was an absolute pleasure." Simon kissed her on both cheeks before turning to Kyle. "Kyle, it has been far too long. I'm still not sure I forgive you for ignoring all my calls. Oh, and Natasha is far too good for you."

As he forged his way through the crowd towards Netta, Natasha blew out a long breath, hand on her chest, and smiled at Kyle. "What a lovely, exhausting man."

"Yes, I'd forgotten how exhausting."

"How long is it since you've seen him?"

Kyle's response was immediate, his gaze straying across the room to where his friend was now engaged in an enthusiastic conversation with the small pharaoh. "Five years."

"Five years? That's a long time. How come?"

For a moment, she thought he wasn't going to answer her but, after the longest pause, he turned back to her with a curiously blank expression. "Work commitments, I guess. Just one of those things, time gets away from you."

Natasha had the distinct impression he had changed his answer at the last second, and wondered what it was he had been about to say. Whatever it had been, it was his business, and she wasn't going to pry. The room was so crowded and noisy it was difficult to hold a civilized conversation, anyway.

The next moment, she was knocked off balance when yet another pharaoh tripped over his own feet, and she found herself stumbling straight into Kyle's arms.

He waved away the man's rather inebriated apologies with a smile. "I should be thanking you. I've been waiting for an excuse to hold Nefertiti in my arms all evening."

Mindful of her resolution to keep her distance and unable to think of a good reason to remain in his embrace, she reluctantly stepped back, disappointed when he immediately released her.

"Come on, why don't we get some air?" His fingers closed around hers and he led her outside, where they found the sundeck to be remarkably empty of guests.

After the noise and heat of the party, the evening air was refreshingly cool, and the sun cast a rosy hue around them as it sank low on the horizon. About to sit in one of the loungers, Natasha looked up in surprise when Kyle's fingers tightened around hers, and he pulled her towards him. Weary of constantly fighting her feelings, she ignored the annoying little voice in the back of her head, and slipped her hands inside his waistcoat so she could rest her face against his chest.

"That's better," he said with some satisfaction, his arms folding around her to pull her even closer. "You've been avoiding me these past couple of days."

"I haven't been avoiding you," she denied softly. She closed her eyes as he rocked gently from side to side, the movement causing his muscles to flex beneath her fingers, sending tingles along her spine.

"Okay, perhaps not avoiding me as such," he agreed. "More a case of avoiding being alone with me. What are you afraid of?"

"I'm not afraid of anything." She lifted her head to deny his words, but instantly realised her mistake when he dropped his head to kiss her.

"Oh, yes you are," he whispered against her lips. "You're frightened you enjoy my kisses too much."

She gazed into his brilliant blue eyes, knowing he spoke the truth, and that he knew it too. What was the point in pretending? She reached up to cup his face. "Kiss me, Kyle."

He willingly obliged and, when she responded without hesitation, what began as a playful kiss quickly escalated and intensified. Abandoning all pretence of holding back, she arched against him as his hand slipped over her hip and up across her ribcage, exploring the curves of her body. The sensations he aroused in her were making her dizzy with longing, and she tugged impatiently at the shirt underneath his waistcoat, wanting to feel his bare skin beneath her fingers. The muscles of his abdomen flickered and clenched at her touch, and he groaned, lifting her slightly as he moved them back along the deck until she came up against the outside wall of the salon.

His mouth left hers to trace a fiery trail of kisses along her throat, over the collar necklace and down to where the swell of her breasts met the top of her dress. She curled her leg around his thigh, her hands slipping around his waist to cup his rounded buttocks, pulling him even closer, desperate to feel him against her.

A shriek of laughter suddenly floated through the open window around the corner of the deck, bringing them to their senses, and she gave a disappointed moan when Kyle broke their kiss and rested his forehead against hers, his eyes closed as he fought to catch his breath and regain his self-control.

"I forgot where I was for a second there." He gave a shaky laugh and eased away from her slightly. When she caught his waistcoat to pull him closer, he gently traced his hand over her stomach to cup her breast once more, and gave her a lingering kiss. "Shall we go somewhere a little more private?"

As he pressed close, there wasn't a single inch of her that didn't tingle with anticipation and need. To hell with her heart, she would deal with that later. Right here, right now, she wanted him, and she was damned well going to have him.

"Yes."

Chapter Nine

"Wait." Natasha hung back when he took her hand and began walking across the deck. "We've only been here an hour or so. I feel bad for leaving so soon."

Kyle slowed his pace and turned back to her with a smile, pulling her into his side and dropping a kiss on her bare shoulder. "I doubt anyone will notice and, besides, I'm not sure I can wait."

She giggled, a thrill of anticipation rippling through her body as she kissed him quickly on the lips before pulling away again. "Only half an hour, please. Some things are worth waiting for, don't you think?"

He closed his eyes with a groan. "Half an hour. Not a minute more."

"Thank you." Stepping closer, she wrapped her arms around his neck and kissed him softly, running her tongue delicately along the line of his lips.

"That is not helping." He clasped her shoulders to gently push her away from him, smiling as he did so. "Wait here. I'll get us something to drink."

Hugging herself with happiness and excitement, she wandered across the sundeck to lean against the railing. Watching the last dying rays of the sun, she was struck by a sudden wave of nausea, and drew in a surprised gasp, holding her hand against her stomach. The feeling passed as suddenly as it came, and she held her breath for a few moments, waiting to see if it returned. When it didn't, she let out a shaky breath. That was a bit odd, but probably a brief reaction to the intensity of feelings Kyle's kisses had stirred in her.

A smile of anticipation curved her lips at the sound of footsteps behind her, and she turned but blinked in surprise when she realised it wasn't who she expected.

"Gemma."

"Hi." Gemma smiled as she came to a halt beside her. "Well, that's quite some outfit. Almost like the real thing."

Natasha stared at her warily. Was that a compliment or an insult? The sharp, sexy tang of Gemma's perfume caused another disconcerting wave of nausea to turn her stomach, but she tried to ignore it and smiled. "Thank you. I like your dress."

"Thanks." The other woman smoothed her hands along the short, cerise shift dress that emphasised her slim, petite figure and shapely legs. "I don't really do fancy dress. It feels…a bit naff." She gave Natasha a quick glance, her expression unreadable.

Natasha nodded as Gemma flicked her shiny, blond bob and stared out across the Nile. "Yes, well, it's not so bad if everyone is wearing it."

Gemma shrugged. "No, I suppose not."

They stood for a minute in silence until Natasha couldn't stand it any longer and turned to leave, but Gemma's voice stopped her.

"Can I talk to you?" She smiled again. "You know, woman to woman?"

Natasha's stomach sank; this was going to be about Kyle. Over the past few days she had completely forgotten about Gemma, had been lulled into a false sense of security. She raised her chin and smiled with a confidence she didn't feel. "Of course."

"Kyle is so lovely, so incredibly kind." Gemma's pale blue eyes gazed into Natasha's earnestly. "You know, he's got such sympathy for…for…" She gestured with her hands as she searched for the word.

"For what?"

"For people less fortunate, people who have suffered, or had it hard…that kind of thing." She gave a shrug. "He's always picking up waifs and strays."

Natasha nodded uncertainly, not sure where she was going with this conversation.

"Look, I would hate for you to get the wrong idea." Gemma laid a cool hand on Natasha's forearm. "I know how easy it is to fall for him, but please, don't mistake his kindness and sympathy for something else."

Natasha's throat was suddenly dry, and she swallowed with difficulty. "Gemma, I…I don't…"

Gemma's sympathetic smile only served to increase her discomfort. "Oh, come on, Natasha. Don't take me for a fool. You wear your heart on your sleeve. Anyone can see you've fallen for him. I don't blame you, I really don't. I guess you could say it was always going to happen if you spent any length of time with him."

Natasha forced herself to meet Gemma's glance when she continued. "I'm not being harsh but, if it were me, I would want to know the truth. I would want someone to tell me." She paused, her eyes narrowing as she looked at Natasha. "And the truth is, he feels sorry for you. You've had it hard. You're an orphan and you've had to bring up your disabled brother on your own. You're what, nearly thirty years old and this is your first holiday abroad?" Gemma paused as she smiled sympathetically. "Kyle is just trying to give you a bit of excitement, a touch of exotic romance."

The burning colour of humiliation that had risen in Natasha's cheeks now seeped away, leaving her mortified.

Oh God, was it true?

Her mind whirled as she tried to think back to the conversations they had had, the kisses they had shared. *'You're on holiday, you should be enjoying yourself.'* That was what Kyle had said the other day just before he kissed her. Was that really what it was all about? Another wave of nausea squirmed in the pit of her stomach, and she pressed the back of her hand against her mouth.

"You've got it wrong. And this isn't my first holiday abroad—" she managed.

"A package holiday lying on a beach in Spain hardly counts to someone like Kyle," Gemma smiled dismissively. "Look, I know it's difficult to hear but, to be honest, you're really not his type." She fished out her phone from her clutch bag to scroll through the photographs. "Look, this is Kyle's type. This is Carrie."

Natasha reluctantly took the phone from her to gaze at the screen. A petite, blonde woman smiled out from the camera. Her pretty almond-shaped eyes held a hint of mischief, and the wide, full-lipped smile suggested a fun personality. Kyle's ex-wife.

She handed the phone back to Gemma without saying a word, but as she did so, she suddenly recognised the resemblance between the two women, with their blonde hair and unusually shaped eyes.

"You see?" Gemma smiled. "Tall, willowy brunettes are just not his thing."

Natasha stared at Gemma's bowed head as she tucked the phone back in her bag, noticing for the first time how dark the roots of her hair were. With a flash of clarity, she suddenly knew the reason for the impractically heavy make-up. Gemma's eyes were not almond-shaped, but the carefully applied kohl helped to make them appear so. And on closer inspection, the bright red lipstick had been applied outside her natural lip-line to make them appear fuller than they really were. Gemma was doing her very best to look like Kyle's ex-wife!

The sympathetic smile only served to increase the nausea turning her stomach in waves, but she forced herself to fight back. She was not some weak, pathetic woman to be pitied, and it was time she stopped acting like one.

"Maybe he's had enough of blondes. After all, Carrie left him. He might be looking for something a bit different."

For a moment, Gemma's eyes widened, and she stared at Natasha in astonishment. "Oh my God. You don't know, do you?" She breathed when she eventually found her voice. "Carrie didn't leave Kyle, you poor fool. She died. He's a widower."

In an instant the world shrank around Natasha, until there was nothing but the two of them; no sound, no air, no boat, just the four-square feet of decking on which they stood. Time seemed to have stopped her heart, too. She stared in horror at Gemma's face, the pale blue eyes incredulous and pitying, her words hanging in the space between them. And then, just as suddenly, the world around them reappeared, and Natasha drew in a strangled breath, covering her mouth with her hand as she turned away in distress.

"Oh no, oh poor Kyle." She had a sudden flashback

to the awful words she had thrown at him that day when they had argued so horribly.

'No wonder your wife left you, Kyle Richardson. You're an arrogant, sanctimonious bastard.'

She closed her eyes in mortification. "I had no idea. I thought they were divorced."

"See what I mean?" Gemma smiled, an unattractive smugness pervading her expression. "If he really felt anything for you, he would have told you."

Still reeling from the news about his wife, Natasha finally saw through Gemma's seemingly friendly advice. Yes, she might be right about Kyle's feelings towards her, about how little she knew him, but it also spoke volumes about how little they knew about her, too. She was not some naïve virgin, living a sheltered life, looking after her poor disabled brother, and trembling at the mere thought of a romantic encounter. She took a deep breath and straightened her shoulders, looking Gemma full in the face.

"I know what you see when you look at me, Gemma. I know you feel sorry for me, and maybe Kyle does, too." She spoke clearly and softly. "But you know, of the two of us, I think you're the one who deserves more pity. At least I am not afraid to be who I am. I can't imagine how exhausting it must be for you, forever trying to be someone you're not, trying to become the image of your boyfriend's former wife. In fact, I feel sorry for both of you. You, because at some point you won't be able to keep up the pretence; and Kyle, because one day he'll wake up and realise you're not the woman he thought you were."

Then, after shaking her head sadly while Gemma simply gaped at her open-mouthed, it was Natasha's turn to offer a sympathetic smile before turning around and walking back into the party.

****

Kyle heaved a sigh of relief when he finally managed to extricate himself from the banal conversation of the small pharaoh Simon had foisted on him with a mischievous grin. The guy didn't know when to shut up. With a glass in each hand, Kyle had been steadily backing away towards the door, nodding and smiling in what he hoped were the right places, all the time itching to get back to Natasha.

Now he turned and caught his breath. There she was, standing hesitantly in the doorway. The effect she had on him was instantaneous. His heart raced at the mere thought of her; actually seeing her had the blood pumping around his body and pounding in his ears so loudly it drowned out all other sound.

As he made his way towards her, his step faltered slightly. She looked pale and anxious, and he frowned, a wave of protectiveness suddenly lending speed to his steps. He was continually amazed by the intensity of the feelings she aroused in him, feelings he was frightened to explore further.

"Hey." He smiled when he reached her side, noting again how pale she looked. When he had left her a short while ago, she had been flushed with happiness and excitement, but now he had a sense of foreboding and wondered what could have happened to effect such a change. "Are you okay?"

"Yes, I'm fine, thank you." She answered politely enough, automatically taking the glass he offered, but he was far from reassured. She was looking at him with a curiously detached expression, almost as if she were seeing him for the first time, and he felt a stab of fear at the coldness in her gaze. "I'm sorry it took me so long. Simon palmed me off on someone who wouldn't shut up."

He slipped his hand around her waist, bewildered by her detachment, and was even more confused when she stepped away from his embrace. He was unsure if she had deliberately moved away from him, or if she had been caught off balance by the group of people squeezing past her in the doorway. He caught her hand and gently pulled her to one side, shocked by how cold her fingers were. Setting his glass down on a table, he began gently chafing her hand between his, bending slightly to catch her downcast gaze.

"You're freezing." He gave her hands a tug, trying a soft laugh. "Hey, come on, it can't be that bad. Will you tell me what's wrong?"

"Nothing's wrong. I'm fine." She gave a cool smile. "I just had time to think, that's all."

"Okay," he answered warily. Aware that her hand was lying limply in his, he tightened his grasp, desperately wanting her to curl her fingers around his but instead she pulled her hand free.

He waited, his mind whirling, wondering what on earth had happened since he left her a few minutes ago. When she eventually lifted her gaze to meet his, he felt his stomach clench at the expression in her eyes. "I've changed my mind."

It didn't come as a surprise. He could have guessed that much from almost the first moment he had seen her standing in the doorway. What he didn't understand was why? He was disappointed, of course he was; he ached for her, but his overwhelming feeling was one of fear.

Fear that he had lost her.

"Natasha, please tell me what's happened. What's wrong?" He lifted a hand to cup her face, but froze when she flinched away from him.

"Why does something have to have happened?" She was suddenly angry. "Am I not allowed to change my mind about wanting to sleep with you?"

"Of course you are," he said, shocked at her outburst. "I don't care about that. All I care about is that something has upset you."

"You don't care about that? Doesn't that just sum it all up? You don't care about not sleeping with me because it's all a game to you, isn't it? Well, I don't need your pity, Kyle Richardson," she hissed, her eyes bright with unshed tears. "I know what you think. Poor, naïve Natasha, let's give her a bit of excitement to keep her going when she's back in her sad, lonely little life in England."

He stared at her, speechless in his confusion. *What the hell was going on?* Behind the anger and resentment, he saw the hurt and fear in her shimmering green eyes. Aware of the curious glances being thrown in their direction, he reached for her hand once again.

"Look, why don't we go outside and talk about this?"

She pushed his hand away, derision twisting her mouth. "My God, are you really so desperate for sex, Kyle? Well, you've no need to worry, there's at least one woman on board this boat who is more than willing to satisfy your urges."

He flinched as if she had slapped him, speechless at the venom with which she had spoken. He made no attempt to follow her when she turned and pushed her way through the crowded room, but his gaze followed her when she joined Nicky on the far side. He shook his head impatiently, narrowing his gaze as he tried unsuccessfully to lip-read her conversation with her brother.

Wine splashed onto his hand as a partygoer jostled into him mumbling an apology, and he glanced down at his as yet untouched glass. Bringing it to his lips, his gaze returned to Natasha, and he deliberately downed the full glass before setting it on the nearest table, and moved purposefully towards her. He needed to find out what was going on.

"Kyle, darling."

The hand on his arm stopped him in mid-stride and he turned impatiently, irritated by this unnecessary delay. He looked down at the petite blonde hanging onto his arm.

"Gemma."

"It's lovely to see you. You look marvellous." She looked up at him through her eyelashes.

"I'm sorry, Gemma, but you'll have to excuse me." He shook off her hand and turned away.

"She's very pretty, isn't she? Your Nefertiti?"

Kyle stopped dead, his gaze fixed on Natasha as she shook her head in response to something Nicky said. He suddenly knew without a doubt that Gemma was the cause of Natasha's upset, and his hands clenched into fists at his side. He turned slowly, shaking with the effort of keeping his anger from showing.

"What did you say to her?" His voice was low and controlled.

"I must admit, I'm a bit surprised at you, Kyle." She shook her head, ignoring his question. "She's not your usual type. I didn't have you down as finding the needy, homely type attractive. I mean, yes, she's pretty enough but she's clearly not up for 'no strings fun', is she? My God, she wouldn't know what to do with you." Gemma gave a tinkling, girlish laugh. "She'd probably run screaming from the bedroom if you so much as tried to unbutton your shirt."

"Gemma, you…" Kyle snapped his mouth shut to stop the stream of vitriol he burned to say, his hands itching at his sides as he fought the urge to shake the woman.

"Oh Kyle, for heaven's sake. Look at yourself. Look at her." Gemma stared at him as if he had lost his mind. "She's not what you need. You know it, I know it, even she knows it."

When she slipped her arms around his waist to rest her head against his chest, he looked down at the blonde head pressed against him and was hit by a sudden flash of clarity. She had no idea what kind of woman Natasha was; that she was vulnerable with an inner core of strength, sensitive but feisty and, by God, she had more sexuality in her little finger than Gemma had in her entire body. He didn't understand what kind of game Gemma was playing, but he didn't want any part of it. He seized her shoulders and thrust her away from him.

"Thank you, Gemma. You've made it all so clear. That woman up there is everything I could ever need, or ever want," he said softly, smiling slightly at her surprised gasp. "And that's exactly why I'm not going to do anything about it."

With that, he turned and walked away, leaving Gemma staring after him.

****

Feeling the beginnings of a headache, Natasha rubbed her forehead and tried to concentrate as Nicky enthusiastically showed her his sketchbook. What a fool she'd been. She should have listened to that stupid little voice in her head, the one that told her to stay away from Kyle. But no, she had decided she knew better. And now, not only had she ended up being hurt, as she knew she would, she had also made a right bloody fool of herself.

She closed her eyes in mortification. A sudden memory of the hurt and bewilderment clouding Kyle's eyes when she had walked away from him sent a stab of regret through her, but she pushed it aside. It served him right for playing with her feelings. Who cares if he thought he was doing her a favour? He was wrong.

Unable to help herself, she glanced across the room, her heart sinking when she saw Gemma slip her arms around Kyle's waist. So, she had been telling the truth. Natasha turned away, tears blurring her vision as disappointment settled in the pit of her stomach. All her defiant words, all her indignant thoughts meant nothing. Once again, she had been lying to herself, hoping against hope that Kyle would prove Gemma wrong. More fool her.

Another sickening lurch of her stomach had beads of sweat breaking out on her upper lip, and she began to panic. The last thing she wanted was to make an even bigger fool of herself by being ill in front of everyone. She swallowed hard against the rising bile in the back of her throat and blinked away her tears, reaching out to touch Nicky's hand, stopping him in mid-flow.

"Nicky, I don't feel very well. I'm going to go back to the boat."

His face fell. "Oh, do I have to come, too?"

"No, of course not. But could you let Aunt Lucy know?"

"All right." His smile faded and was replaced by a frown. "Are you okay?"

She managed a faint smile. "Yes, I'm fine. I just feel a bit queasy. You have a good time."

Choosing the exit furthest away from Kyle, Natasha swiftly made her way off the boat, breaking into a run along the riverbank and up the steps to the *Aten's Dream*. She only just made it to her cabin in time, sinking to her knees in the en-suite bathroom, before being violently sick.

The pounding in her head made her dizzy, and she knelt on the floor for a few minutes, concentrating on breathing slowly and deeply in an attempt to prevent any further vomiting. After a while, desperate to rid herself of the sour taste in her mouth, she grasped the hand basin and pulled herself to her feet, leaning over the basin to splash cold water over her face and rinse out her mouth.

With some effort, she turned slowly to make the few steps into the bedroom, noticing the door to the corridor was still open after her hurried entrance. Pushing it closed, she turned and quickly undressed, no sooner pulling on her vest and shorts before she was overcome by the certain knowledge she was going to vomit again, and hurried once more into the bathroom.

Chapter Ten

The door flew open as Kyle strode into the salon, and Nicky and Lucy looked up from their breakfast in surprise. His mood darkened considerably when he saw Natasha was not with them.

"Morning, Kyle." Lucy beamed at him. "Wasn't it a lovely party last night? Lots of old faces and plenty of catching up to do."

"Where's Natasha?" He had not slept well, and was in no mood for pleasantries. His thoughts had been full of Natasha, wondering what it was Gemma had said to her. Unhappily aware that his feelings for her were growing stronger every day, he had even tried to convince himself that she was nothing but a tease, leading him on and then turning him away at the last moment. That had given him a focus for his anger, but only for a few short minutes; he knew that was not her style.

His anger had then shifted to the fact she had not given him a chance to defend himself, running off before he could give his side of the story, whatever that story was. It hurt that whatever Gemma had told her, Natasha had obviously believed it instantly, not even giving him the benefit of the doubt. And now, this morning, she was hiding, acting like a sulky teenager.

"She might still be poorly," said Nicky, oblivious to Kyle's ill temper. "She left the party early last night

140

because she didn't feel very well."

Kyle turned on his heel with a disbelieving snort, only just managing not to slam the door behind him. Marching down the corridor, he took a deep, steadying breath before coming to a halt and knocking on Natasha's door.

"Natasha." He waited for a few seconds, listening for sounds of movement but heard nothing. He forced himself to speak evenly. "Natasha, please open the door."

When there were no sounds from within, he lost patience and rapped on the door with the palm of his hand. "Look, this is ridiculous. Open the damn door."

He wondered briefly if he should leave her to it, but then remembered the words she had flung in his face last night, and his anger and frustration returned to the surface. "If you don't open the door, I'm coming in and I don't give a damn if you're decent or not."

He rattled the door handle, fully expecting it to be locked but, to his surprise, it opened, and he walked in. The bed was neatly made, complete with her Nefertiti crown and dress draped over one corner.

Had she got up earlier and was already on the sundeck without anyone realising?

He looked around in confusion but, when his glance reached the en-suite, his heart skipped a beat, and the breath left his body in a sharp gasp.

Natasha lay slumped on the floor, her back against the wall and her legs splayed out in front of her.

"Natasha. What the—?" He rushed across the room and dropped to his knees next to her, gently lifting her face to his.

He drew in a deep breath, shocked by her

appearance. Her eyes were closed, her skin ashen, with tear tracks running through the mascara that had smudged around her eyes. Her lips were colourless.

"Natasha." His eyes raked over her face while his fingers gently felt her head, searching for any sign that she had fallen and hurt herself, and might be unconscious but, at the sound of his voice, her eyes fluttered open.

"Kyle." Her voice was a mere whisper. "I'm sorry, I couldn't get to the door."

"Did you fall? Are you hurt?" He cupped her face with his hand when her eyes began to close once more.

She gave the tiniest shake of her head. "No, couldn't stop being sick."

"You've been here all night?" He pressed a hand to her forehead, wincing at the heat radiating from her skin, and briefly stood to open the small window to let in some air before resuming his place beside her. "How long since you were last sick?"

Her eyes had closed again, and he grimaced before touching her shoulder in an attempt to rouse her. "Natasha. How long since you were last sick?"

A frown crossed her forehead. "I don't know. I've lost track of time. Maybe an hour." With an effort she managed to open her eyes and focus on him, the merest hint of a smile curving her lips. "I don't think there can be anything left in me."

"Right." He slipped his arms around her shoulders and beneath her knees, carefully lifting her from the floor. The movement must have aggravated her ribs, sore from hours of heaving over the toilet as well as lying all night on the floor, because she gave a soft groan. Murmuring an apology, Kyle dropped a gentle kiss on her forehead as he carried her through to the bedroom, and laid her down on the bed.

Reaching into the ottoman beneath the window, he pulled out a clean white sheet and draped it over her, but she didn't stir and already appeared to be asleep. Feeling her forehead once again, he pulled the sheet down to her waist, and opened the cabin window before flicking on the overhead fan.

He paused to stand over her for a few seconds, chewing his lip as a wave of protectiveness swept over him. She would probably sleep for a good while, but what if she were ill again?

****

Natasha gradually became aware of the gentle roll of the boat, and the realisation they were under sail filtered through her sleep-fogged brain. She frowned, reluctant to open her eyes, and wanting nothing more than to drift back to sleep. However, the sounds of children playing, and men shouting floated in through the open window, and these sounds of everyday life pulled her into full wakefulness. She unwillingly opened her eyes, then blinked in surprise for several long moments, trying to work out why Kyle was in her room. He was sitting on the small sofa beneath the window, a pile of papers on his knee and his face a picture of concentration.

What was he doing in her cabin, and why were they sailing already? Had she slept in?

Blinking away the last remnants of sleep, the events of the previous evening came flooding back and she unconsciously held her breath, trying to determine if she still felt ill.

Exhausted, yes; very empty, not surprising; but nauseous? No, thank goodness. But that didn't explain why he was sitting in her cabin.

"Kyle?"

He looked up immediately, his expression softening, and he put the papers to one side before moving to sit beside her on the bed.

"Hey." He gently brushed her hair away from her face. "Welcome back to the land of the living."

"How long have I been asleep?" She lifted a hand to rub her eyes, wincing at the heavy feeling in her arms.

"About six hours which, considering you spent the entire night in the bathroom, is probably not quite long enough yet."

Stifling a yawn, she glanced at her fingers and saw they were black from the mascara she had not removed last night. Both hands flew to her face, feeling for and finding the remnants of eyeliner and mascara all around her eyes and tracking across her cheeks. Colour flooded her face, and she rolled away from Kyle, covering her face with her hands.

"Oh God, don't look at me," she wailed, her voice muffled against her hands. "I must look a sight."

He gave a soft chuckle, and she felt the mattress lift when he stood up. "I'm taking that as a sign you're feeling a little better."

She didn't move, but heard him rummaging around in the en-suite before returning to sit on the bed.

"Come here, turn around."

"No."

She felt his fingers gently grasp her forearm as he pulled her around to face him.

"Look at me."

She shook her head, hands still covering her face, and jumped when he gently prised them away.

"Will you stop being so vain?" He grinned at her. "I've seen worse."

To her complete surprise, he reached across to the bedside table and picked up a cotton wool pad, drenching it in makeup remover, before cradling her face with one hand and gently smoothing the pad over her eyes with the other. Her initial discomfort faded as he continued to cleanse her face of make-up, gently wiping the moist cotton wool across her cheeks, forehead and chin with soft, soothing strokes until she felt herself drifting back to sleep.

This time when she awoke, the first thing she became aware of was the familiar scent of Kyle's aftershave giving her prior warning of his proximity. So, when she opened her eyes and saw him lying fully clothed on the bed, she was not surprised. In fact, her heart gave a disconcerting leap, and she couldn't prevent a smile from curving her lips. What she wouldn't give to wake up to the sight of him every morning.

She tried to stay as still as possible, reluctant to disturb the moment, but he must have sensed she was awake. He turned his head to glance at her, smiling when he saw her looking at him.

"Hey."

"Hey." She returned his smile, stretching out her arms, stiff from hours spent lying in bed. "What time is it?"

He checked his watch. "Just gone seven in the evening. How are you feeling?"

"Better." She rubbed her eyes, trying to brush away the last remnants of sleep, before sitting up to shuffle back in the bed so she could lean against the headboard. "Empty, a bit shaky. But okay, I think."

"Good." To her disappointment, Kyle swung himself from the bed and reached for the bottle of mineral water sitting on the bedside table. He poured a glass and held it out to her. "Here, drink this, you're going to be dehydrated."

She looked at him warily. "I don't want to start being sick again."

He handed her the glass. "I don't think you will. You've gone over twelve hours now, so you should be fine. You've had a minor bout of the famous 'Pharaoh's revenge', I'm afraid."

"Minor bout?" She took the glass reluctantly and sipped the water. "Didn't feel very minor to me."

He grinned, sitting down on the sofa beneath the window. "I'm sure it didn't, but people can suffer from it for a few days, so it's good that you seem to be recovering okay. You've given Nicky quite a scare, though. He's desperate to see you."

Natasha nodded, with a frown. "Yes, I suppose I must have. I'll get up in a minute. I think I've spent more than enough time in bed."

The silence between them lengthened until Kyle spoke quietly.

"What did she say to you?"

Her heart sank. She'd been trying not to think about last night, and now she closed her eyes wearily, wondering whether or not to pretend she didn't understand what he meant. *But what would be the point in that?* Instead, she shook her head. "It doesn't matter."

"It does matter," he insisted softly. He leaned forward, elbows resting on his knees, to catch her gaze with his. "It matters a great deal."

"Kyle…" She broke off with a sigh. *What could she*

tell him? Her stomach squirmed, but this time with humiliation rather than nausea, as she remembered Gemma's assertion that Kyle's actions were as a result of pity and kindness rather than real attraction. Was that why he was here now?

"Natasha. Please."

"Okay, okay." She shifted uncomfortably before turning to face him, bringing her legs up to cross them beneath the cotton sheet. *How did she explain what had happened last night?*

She could feel her cheeks begin to burn, remembering the words Gemma had spoken so casually, and blew out a long, soft breath to try and steady her breathing, looking up at Kyle as she did so. He simply returned her gaze, waiting patiently, giving her time.

"She said a lot of things. But the gist of it was, that I should stay away from her boyfriend, that you feel sorry for me, and are trying to give me a bit of excitement, so I can look back and be grateful when I'm living my sad, dreary little life back in England."

She didn't attempt to hide the bitterness she felt, and waited for Kyle's reaction to her bald statement. His utter stillness told her she had shocked him, that whatever he had been expecting, it hadn't been that. She started in surprise when he suddenly stood, as if unable to contain whatever emotion he was feeling.

He turned from her and ran a hand through his hair, shaking his head, and his shoulders lifted when he drew in a long, long breath before turning back to her.

"Right." He held up a hand as if to prevent her from speaking, but it was completely unnecessary. She realised that she was holding her own breath and waiting for his response, leaving herself open once again to humiliation as she waited desperately for him to prove Gemma wrong.

"Gemma is not, and never has been, my girlfriend. We had a brief…fling, whatever you want to call it, over a year ago. So, I don't know what game she is playing, but…"

He spun away from her again to pace the short distance to the cabin door and back, and Natasha could sense his frustration, his confusion. After a moment he moved to stand in front of her, before squatting down so that his eyes were on a level with hers. He gave a crooked smile and reached to take her hands in his.

"And as for feeling sorry for you." He gave a soft laugh and dropped his head, leaving her staring at the shiny, dark hair, and wishing she could run her fingers through it. Her hands must have automatically moved at the mere thought, because his fingers tightened around hers and he lifted his head, causing her heart to thump in her chest at the intensity of his gaze. "I don't understand what it is about you that I should feel sorry for. You make me feel a lot of things; a lot of things I really don't want to feel, but not one of those is pity."

Hope soared through her at his words, and she couldn't help herself. "What sort of things?"

He didn't answer her directly. "When I kiss you, it's because I can't help myself, and I want you so badly it hurts, but it's more than that. I care about you, Natasha."

The way he said those words caused a stab of fear to shoot through her, and the fledgling hope began to crumble.

"You say that like it's a bad thing." She tried a smile, but it faded when he simply looked at her.

"It is for some people…for me."

"I don't understand." To her dismay, tears filled her eyes and she looked away. *He cared about her; how could that be a bad thing?*

"I don't want to care about you. I don't want to care about anyone." He smiled to soften the words. "In just under a week's time your holiday is going to be over, you'll go back to England and your life, and I'll stay here in Egypt and get on with my life. We'll never see each other again."

"It doesn't have to be like that."

Again, he gave that soft, humourless, heartbreaking laugh. He still held her hands in his, and now he squeezed them before bringing them to his lips and kissing her knuckles. "Yes, it does."

"But, last night…" She was unable to stop the words, and wished she could just shut up and accept what he was saying with dignity. But she couldn't. He said he cared for her, so there was still hope, still hope she could persuade him that it didn't have to end.

"Last night I couldn't help myself, and I can't guarantee that, put in the same situation over the next few days, I would be able to say no to you if you asked me to kiss you like you did last night," he said honestly. "But it still wouldn't make any difference when the time comes for you to leave. I will still let you walk away from me when you go back to England. I won't follow you, and I don't want you to stay. I have nothing to offer you, Natasha, not in the long term. Is that really what you want? Could you settle for that?"

"Yes." She held his gaze defiantly and, even though she felt like crying, couldn't help but smile when he raised his eyebrows in disbelief. Her shoulders dropped. "No. I would want more."

His gaze flickered at her honesty, and she saw him swallow, closing his eyes briefly, before smiling at her. "I know."

She looked down at her hands in his, blinking away hot tears as she concentrated on breathing. He had always been straight with her, had never hinted that he wanted a relationship, but it had not stopped her from secretly dreaming and hoping. Despite trying to convince herself otherwise, she was falling in love with him. Those hopes were now reduced to crumbling ruins, much like Akhenaten's beloved city.

But she was aware of his gaze upon her, and could only hope that he hadn't guessed the depth of her feelings for him. She was determined he never would; she would carry on as she always did, and grieve in private.

She suddenly looked up at him with a slight smile. "You do know she's in love with you, don't you?"

He frowned at the swift change of subject. "What?"

"Gemma. She's in love with you."

He shook his head with a knowing smile, squeezing her hands one last time before straightening up, and moving to sit on the sofa. "Now that's where you're wrong. She's not into commitment. That's why it worked for a while."

It was Natasha's turn to smile knowingly at him. Men could be so naïve sometimes. "That's exactly what she wanted you to think. She knew you weren't interested in a long-term relationship, so she gave you exactly what you wanted. But, always with the hope you would fall in love with her."

"No." He shook his head vehemently. "No, she was more than clear."

"Of course, she was. Otherwise, you'd have been off

like a shot." Natasha held her hands up in frustration at his dimness. "So why did she turn up out of the blue earlier in the week, trying to invite herself on to your boat? And again at the party last night? Do you really believe her when she said she was just passing through?"

He frowned. "It was a bit unlikely." He stood up, running his fingers through his hair, and turned his gaze to her. "Do you really think so?"

She rolled her eyes. "Yes."

He heaved a sigh and shoved his hands in his pockets. "It does explain a few things, I guess." He stared out of the window. "Well, she might feel a little differently today. I was a bit short with her last night. I can't see her being under any illusions about my feelings for her now. I might have been a bit harsh, to be honest."

"Then you should apologise to her."

He turned around in surprise. "After everything she said to you, you still want me to be kind to her?"

She gave a rueful smile. "Love has a tendency to make us say and do things we wouldn't ordinarily do. She only said those things to me because she was desperately afraid of losing you. The fact that you don't love her isn't her fault."

She understood those feelings only too well, but lifted her head and gave him a bright smile, one that hopefully belied her pain. "So, what do we do now?"

He frowned slightly, but moved to sit beside her on the bed. He put his arm around her shoulders. "Well. We could pretend last night never happened. You get your lazy self out of bed, go up to reassure Nicky that you're not dying, and we carry on with making sure you have the best holiday of your life."

He hooked a finger underneath her chin and turned

151

her to face him. After a moment's hesitation, he dropped his head and caught her lips in the sweetest, most heart-breaking kiss of her life, before drawing back and resting his forehead against hers. "And I work on making sure I never do that again."

He was reaching for the cabin door when she suddenly remembered what else Gemma had said to her last night.

"Kyle." She waited until he turned around, his fingers resting on the door handle. "Gemma...she told me about Carrie."

He stiffened slightly, but his gaze didn't waver from hers, and she carried on in a rush. "I'm so sorry for what I said to you the other night. I had no idea, I thought you were divorced, and what I said was horrible. I didn't mean it...I'm sorry."

"I think we both said a lot of things we regret." After a moment's hesitation, he gave a lopsided grin. "Although, I think perhaps you might have had a point about the arrogant, sanctimonious bastard bit."

With that, he was gone, leaving her alone once again, staring at the door when he closed it behind him.

Chapter Eleven

"Tash!" Nicky ran across the deck when she appeared at the top of the stairs, her hair still damp from the shower. He stopped short of her, his hands plucking at the edge of his t-shirt, a sure sign he was worried about something. "How are you feeling?"

"Much better." She gave a bright smile to reassure him, putting her arm through his and walking across to where Lucy was snoozing in one of the reclining sun loungers. She sank gratefully into one of the rattan chairs, aware of Nicky's constant gaze.

"Are you sure you're okay?"

"Yes, Nicky, I'm fine. I had a tummy bug, that's all."

"But, do you think it was because I didn't wash the fruit properly? Do you think I left some germs on them?" His bottom lip trembled as he voiced the fear that had obviously been swirling around his head since this morning.

"Oh Nicky, no. No, I don't think it was that at all, please stop worrying." She leaned across to touch her younger brother's arm. "To tell you the truth, I think it was more likely to be something I picked up from Colin the camel, from his reins or something. They didn't look very clean, did they?"

He shook his head vehemently, his relief palpable. "No, they didn't. Mine were really dirty."

"There you are then. I think it's very likely I picked up my bug from that." As she leaned back in the chair, her stomach gave a growl of hunger, and she giggled in surprise. "I think my tummy is trying to say that it's very empty."

As if on cue, Nader appeared carrying a tray, which he placed on the table in front of her. The tray held a jug of fresh water, tinkling with ice cubes and slices of fresh lemon, a plate of pita breads, and a large bowl of hummus.

"You should eat something, Miss Morgan."

"Oh, Nader, thank you very much. I am hungry, but…" She didn't wish to offend him, but was frightened of risking further illness.

"You need not worry." He smiled in understanding. "This is very gentle on your stomach; no sickness." He nodded and gestured for her to eat.

"Thank you, that's really kind." She poured herself a glass of water before breaking off a small piece of pita bread and dipping it into the hummus. It tasted divine and, as the first mouthful hit her stomach, she realised she was indeed ravenously hungry.

Two pita breads later, she pushed the tray away and rubbed her stomach ruefully, but this time feeling satisfied rather than nauseous. "So, Nicky, tell me what you did today."

Relieved to see his sister fully recovered, Nicky pulled his chair close to Natasha's and pulled out his book, keen to show her the sketches he had made. "Aunty Lucy and me went to Abydos this morning." He looked up, suddenly worried. "Kyle said we still ought to go, even though you were poorly, because we had to start sailing again this afternoon. He said we couldn't wait until tomorrow because we had to keep to the timetable for…tides…and to get to Luxor ready for our plane. You don't mind, do you?"

"Of course not. I didn't expect you all to sit up here all day doing nothing." She pointed to his sketchpad. "Come on, you can show me what I missed."

****

It had been two days since the party, and Natasha was feeling much better; another full day of sailing yesterday as they made their way along the Nile to Qena had allowed her to rest on the sun deck, chatting and reminiscing with Lucy in the shade, although the day was slightly cooler and more bearable than previously. Kyle popped up every so often to share a drink or a meal, his manner easy and relaxed as he occasionally ran a gentle finger along Natasha's arm or chin, but for the most part it was just the two women.

Today, though, she was itching to explore once again, and as she leaned against the railing, waiting impatiently for Mac to arrive with the Jeep, she determined to enjoy the last two days of her holiday. A short blast of a car horn brought a smile to her face when Mac arrived, and she made her way quickly to the gangplank, eager and excited to be leaving the boat after the last two days of forced relaxation. Kyle was already standing on the bank of the Nile, and held out his hand to help her, his expression hidden behind sunglasses. When she took his hand and stepped onto the dusty ground, he caught her other hand in his, and gently pulled her a little closer.

"Are we okay?" he asked softly.

She looked up at him, but saw only her own reflection in the mirror-like glasses. Right at this moment, with her hands in his, there was nowhere else on this earth she would rather be. Nor did she want to spoil the moment, not when his concern for her was evident in the roughness of his voice. "We're good," she said.

He lifted her hands to his lips, kissing her knuckles, before turning away and walking with her to the waiting car, his hand still loosely clasped around hers.

"Come on, slow coach," he threw over his shoulder to Nicky, who was making his way from the boat.

Having visited Dendera on many occasions over the years, Lucy had opted to stay behind on the boat and, as a result, it was the three of them. The walled complex at the site was truly breathtaking, particularly the temple dedicated to Hathor. Almost every available surface was covered in hieroglyphs and friezes describing ancient stories that had been passed down through the ages, and which Kyle translated for them. After a while, Nicky wandered off on his own to find a quiet corner where he could draw.

Dendera was a little busier than some of the other sites they had visited so far, with a few tourists wandering around, but still not as busy as Natasha had anticipated. She enjoyed listening to Kyle as he talked her through the history of the different temples, her hand still loosely encased in his. She resolutely refused to dwell on the fact that in a couple of days' time, she would be on her way home and all this would be over. She would never see him again, never feel his hand in hers, never hear his voice.

The sun rose higher in the sky, beating down with intensity, and she pulled out her water bottle, taking a long satisfying drink. She glanced across the site to where Nicky was still perched on a low wall, and caught his eye, raising the bottle to ask if he wanted some. He shook his head and reached into his bag to pull out his own bottle, and she turned away, reassured. At that moment, a young American couple approached Kyle to ask if he would take a photograph of the two of them. When he handed back their camera, they indicated they had overheard him talking and he appeared to be very knowledgeable about the place. Before he knew it, Kyle found himself engaged in conversation with them.

Smiling to herself, Natasha moved off to explore the site on her own, wandering without any real purpose, and taking a few photographs. Unlike the temple of Hathor, which was incredibly well preserved, many of the other temples and buildings across this site had been reduced to a series of crumbling walls, only able to hint at their former glory. Thinking she might get a bit of height and perspective to her photographs, she climbed the steps to one of the many derelict temples and stood, hands on hips, breathing heavily from the slight exertion.

She was unable to prevent the smile curving her lips at the sight that met her. Egypt was everything she had ever hoped for, and she gazed around her, determined not to forget a single part of it. The sun beating down on her shoulders brought the realisation that the heat really was getting too much, a sure sign they should be thinking about making their way back to the boat.

Skipping lightly down the steps, Natasha saw Nicky putting away his sketchbook and, as he looked across at her, she lifted her hand and tapped her watch. It was time to go. He nodded and began making his towards her.

She had almost reached the bottom when her bag slipped from her shoulder. Twisting to catch the bag, she stumbled and missed the last step, taking two awkwardly long strides forward in an effort to regain her balance. Gravity took the upper hand when she tipped forwards and landed in a rather ungraceful heap. Winded from the heavy landing, she lay for a few moments trying to catch her breath, gritting her teeth with embarrassment, and hoping no-one had seen her fall.

****

Kyle finally managed to excuse himself from the American couple, and turned around to look for Natasha. Drawing a sharp breath, he realised the person lying in a crumpled heap at the bottom of the steps was Natasha, and his heart stopped for one, painful second, before starting again with a mighty thump in his chest. Black spots swam across his vision while the blood roared in his ears, drowning out all other sound, and he found himself unable to move, unable to do anything other than stare at the motionless form lying on the ground.

"No." An agonised moan escaped his lips as the memory of another time, another body lying in a similar position at the bottom of the stairs forced its way into his thoughts. Except that time the figure had blonde hair.

When Nicky ran across to Natasha, the movement brought Kyle back to the present, and released his temporary inability to move. He sprinted towards them, muttering under his breath. "Not again. Please, not again."

Nicky was slightly ahead, and reached her first but, instead of reaching down to help, he bent double with laughter, and pointed at her. "Tash, that was awesome. I wish I'd had my phone out. I could have recorded you and put it on YouTube."

Kyle skidded to a halt beside them, his breath

coming in short, painful gasps. He blinked hard, his legs shaking so badly he feared they might give way at any moment.

"Oh thanks, Nicky, very funny." Natasha grinned up at her brother, reaching for his hand. "Here, help me up before I die of embarrassment."

"No, no." Kyle stepped in front of Nicky, and dropped to his knees beside her. "Look, don't move. Are you hurt? Did you bang your head?"

He looked around, swallowing down the panic rising in his chest. He needed to get help, needed to make sure. "Don't move, I'll call an ambulance or a doctor or something."

Natasha stared at him from where she lay on the dusty ground. "Don't be ridiculous. Help me up."

"No, I mean it. Don't move." He lifted a trembling hand to brush sand away from her cheek. "We need to get you checked out."

"Oh, for heaven's sake." She knocked his hand away in irritation, and attempted to get to her feet, but Kyle's hand on her shoulder kept her on the ground.

"Stay there while I get someone to check you over." Deathly pale, he shook his head impatiently while he fished for the phone tucked in his jeans pocket.

Unable to prevent the tremor in his fingers, he swore beneath his breath when he misdialled, and tried again, but before he could connect the call, Natasha snatched the phone from him.

"What is the matter with you?" She hissed angrily. "I am perfectly all right; I don't need checking over."

Scrambling to her feet, acutely aware that a number of tourists were eyeing them curiously, she backed away from him with a look of disbelief.

"You shouldn't get up…" Kyle reached out to take her arm. "Look, let's sit down over there."

He tried to lead her back to the steps, but Natasha dragged her arm from his.

"Back off. I missed a step, that's all."

He flinched at the look in her eyes, the one that told him she thought he was acting crazy, and he turned to Nicky for support, but quickly looked away at the uneasy confusion he saw in the younger man's gaze. Kyle took a couple of steps backward, pulling off his hat to drag his fingers through his hair, confusion and fear swirling round his head in equal measures.

After a few moments, he turned and walked away, without any clear idea where he was going, only that he needed to get a grip.

****

Mac automatically started up the Jeep when Kyle flung open the door and got in.

"Are the others on their way?"

Kyle stared through the window without responding, still trying to make sense of everything.

"Kyle, I said are the others on their way?"

"Dammit, Mac." He slammed open the door and strode down the road a few paces to stand there, taking long, deep breaths in an effort to stem the panic that had been trying to force its way to the surface ever since he had seen Natasha lying on the ground.

It had almost happened again.

He drew in a shuddering breath and closed his eyes, feeling dangerously close to tears.

It was a warning. He should have learned by now.

Ten minutes later, he heard them making their way to the Jeep, heard Nicky calling his name, but he ignored him and instead heard Natasha telling Nicky to leave it. Without looking at any of them, he returned to the vehicle, and tersely told Mac to get a move on.

****

Later that evening, Kyle sat on the banks of the Nile, watching the sun slowly sink into the horizon while he absently threw pebbles into the river. On arrival back at the boat, he had immediately gone below deck, and set about getting ready to sail for Luxor, relieved when Nicky had not sought him out as he had feared. Now moored for the night, he had gone out for a walk while the others ate their evening meal and, rather than return to the boat, he sought solitude here on the bank, trying to quell the fear that threatened to overwhelm him; fear that, once again, history would repeat itself.

Shaking his head at that thought, he picked up another pebble, and threw it viciously into the water. *Idiot!* He'd known the danger, had recognised that Natasha was different, that she made him feel differently. Yet he'd carried on, lying to himself about how deep he was falling, convincing himself it was only a bit of fun, that he didn't care for her. And even when he eventually admitted to himself he did care, still he hadn't walked away. He had continued to lie, to tell himself he could switch off his feelings for her, keep things platonic. He was nothing more than a damned fool, one who should have known better.

****

Natasha walked slowly towards him, faltering slightly when he glanced up before turning away again to throw a stone into the Nile. She had no idea what had caused his uncharacteristic behaviour earlier, but she intended to find out. Without a word, she sat down beside him, and drew up her legs to rest her chin on her knees. They sat in silence for several long minutes before eventually he spoke.

"Are you okay?" His voice was casual, but the stillness of his body told her he was worried.

"I'm fine. A bit of a bruised elbow, but other than that, it was more my pride that was damaged." She frowned, aware of the tension within him, but completely confused as to what was causing it. "I'm sorry I worried you, but I just missed the last step. That was all. It wasn't a big deal."

After a further pause, she tried to dig further. "Will you tell me what that was all about this afternoon?" Her voice was soft and non-accusatory.

For a long moment, he didn't respond, and continued throwing his stones. She waited patiently, until he finally threw in the last one and turned to face her.

"I over-reacted."

She gave a soft, surprised laugh. "I'll say."

"I'm sorry." His gaze swept her face, as if committing it to memory, and the pain shining from his eyes made the breath still in the back of her throat.

"Kyle, what is it?" Her fingers curled around his arm. "Tell me. Please."

"Carrie." He swept a weary hand across his face, rubbing his palm against the dark stubble. "She was...I don't know, carrying laundry down the stairs, I guess. I came home from work and found her lying on the floor in the hall. She'd fallen down the stairs and banged her head. Such a stupid, little thing. She never regained consciousness."

"Oh Kyle." Natasha closed her eyes with dawning

understanding, and leaned in close to rest her head on his arm. "I'm so sorry. This afternoon brought it all back."

He shook his head. "It's not just that."

She straightened to look at him, the expression on his face somehow filling her with dread.

"Today was a warning. One last chance, maybe," he said, his gaze fixed on the horizon. "It isn't just Carrie. It's been everyone I ever loved or cared about. They all died. They always die."

He shrugged in a matter-of-fact way. "And by lying to myself and to you about how I feel about you, by pretending I don't care, that it's nothing serious, I've put you in danger."

She looked at him warily.

"I've lost everyone; my parents, my brother, my best friend at school, Carrie, Joe…I've lost them all. It's my fault, and I won't lose you, too."

"I don't understand. How is it your fault?"

"Because everyone I care about dies." He turned to look at her then, with a strangely distant gaze. "I know how it sounds and I don't expect you to believe me, but it is true, and I live with it. Today was proof, if you needed it. I know I certainly don't."

"Today was proof of nothing other than that I'm really clumsy," she said in exasperation. "It was one step. I fell down one step."

He didn't respond, and she sat beside him quietly, trying to take in everything he had told her. Her heart ached for him; knowing and sharing the pain of losing both parents. *But to think that it was his fault?* She turned to him once more, moving to sit facing him, and taking his hands in hers.

"Look, Kyle, I can't pretend to know what you've

had to go through, losing so many people you love, but…I do know what it's like to lose your parents. It's been twelve years since mum and dad's accident, and I still miss them and think of them every day. It still hurts." Her voice trembled, and she swallowed hard with unexpected emotion as she thought of her parents.

He leaned forward and clasped her shoulders gently, ducking his head to meet her gaze. "I know," he said softly. "I know."

She shook her head, blinking away her tears. "But to think it's your fault? That's just crazy. People die, Kyle. They die all the time, and some people have more people they care about die than others. But it's no-one's fault; it's just chance, fate, whatever you want to call it. It's not anything that you have caused."

He dropped his hands from her shoulders with a slight shake of his head, and she could sense his emotional retreat from her, sense his disbelief. She was helpless in the face of such determination.

"Well, I don't believe I'm in any danger. I care about you, Kyle, and I won't pretend that I don't." She cupped his face with her hands and kissed him. For a few sweet seconds he kissed her back, desperately, hungrily, but the next moment he pushed her away from him and scrambled to his feet, turning away from her, and dragging his hand through his hair.

"Dammit, Natasha, don't."

"Kyle, this is ridiculous," she snapped, her helplessness giving way to anger. "Okay, so this…this curse, shall we call it? This curse. Is it a distance thing then?"

He turned back to her, visibly confused, and caught off guard by her unexpected question. "What do you mean?"

"Well, you seem to think that once I'm back home in England, I'll be perfectly safe. So, is it a distance thing then? How far is far enough, do you think?"

He sighed at the thinly veiled sarcasm. "Funny. No, it's nothing to do with distance. I've told you—"

"Yes, you've told me. It's anyone you care about." She held his gaze defiantly. "Let's be clear about that then, shall we?"

She could see him looking at her warily, obviously unsure where she was going with this.

"All this is because you claim I'm in danger because you care about me so much." She waited until he gave the merest hint of a nod. "Well then, me being back at home in England shouldn't make any difference, should it? Not if you care about me as much as you say you do."

She gave a bitter smile as her words hit home, and she carried on. "So, the fact that you are so sure I'll be safe once this holiday is over, is that, from your point of view, out of sight is out of mind. Not much of a vote of confidence in the strength of your feelings for me, is it?"

Her anger suddenly dissipated, and she got to her feet, once again taking his hands in hers. "Kyle, I don't believe in any curse, and I'm not afraid. But don't you see, even if this curse did exist, pushing me away wouldn't make any difference? Don't you think I should have a say in what happens next?"

The look in his eyes broke her heart when he pulled his hands from hers. "I'm sorry, Natasha, but no I don't. I can't go through it again. I won't."

Chapter Twelve

Natasha lay on the bed, tears slowly trickling down her cheek and onto the pillow as she sobbed quietly. Her emotions were so mixed up, she didn't know if she was crying because of Kyle's determination to avoid his feelings, or because she felt the loss of her parents more keenly today. She didn't move when she heard the gentle tap on her door.

"Tash?" Nicky knocked a little louder. "Tash, are you in there?"

"I'm here."

He opened the door, stopping just inside when he saw her lying motionless on her side. "Are you okay? Are you poorly again?"

"No, I'm not poorly." Her voice was flat, and she heard the door close when Nicky moved uncertainly into the room.

He sat down on the small sofa, looking at her with a worried expression. "What's up?"

She looked at her younger brother, at his innocent, open face, and immediately felt guilty for causing him to worry. "I'm okay. A bit sad, that's all."

"Sad?" He frowned. "Why are you sad? Aren't you enjoying your holiday?"

She passed a hand across her cheeks, wiping away her tears. "Yes, I'm enjoying my holiday but...I don't know. For some reason I really miss Mum and Dad today."

A single tear traced from the corner of her eye down to her ear and onto the pillow. "Do you remember them, Nicky? Do you ever miss them?"

After a pause, he nodded, his mouth turning downwards a little as his face clouded slightly. He glanced down at his wrist, plucking at the watch he always wore, and with a jolt of surprise, Natasha remembered it had belonged to their father. Nicky's face brightened as he gently fingered the leather strap. "I do get sad sometimes, but then I think about my happy memories, and it makes me not sad anymore."

"That sounds a good idea." She pulled the pillow a little closer, and snuggled into it, smiling at her brother. "Tell me your happy memories."

His face broke into a grin, and he leaned forward. "Well, remember when you used to go ice skating every Saturday morning?" He waited for her to nod her confirmation. "Me and Dad used to walk down to the harbour and look at all the boats, and then we'd walk back to that little café. I'd get a waffle with squirty cream and strawberry sauce, and a hot chocolate with marshmallows and chocolate sprinkles. Dad always had a bacon sandwich and a cup of tea. I loved Saturday mornings."

Natasha sat up, drawing up her legs to rest her chin on her knees, her mood lifting as she joined in with his reminiscences. "And Sundays were our family day out. We'd all pile in the car and drive up to the moors, or some little village in the middle of nowhere."

Nicky nodded enthusiastically. "And mum always brought a picnic."

"Egg sandwiches!" They both said in unison, before

breaking out into laughter.

"See? You're happy now."

Natasha smiled. "You're right. Next time I'm sad, I'll think about my happy memories."

There was a pause as Nicky looked at her carefully. "So, will you come upstairs with the others? We're playing board games, but it's not the same if you're not there. And it's nearly our last day. We'll be going home soon."

She looked at his naïve, eager face, and laughed softly. "Yes, I'll come up in five minutes." She ran her hands across her tousled hair. "I'll just freshen up first."

****

Staring at her reflection as she brushed her long, dark hair, Natasha wondered about Nicky's inexhaustibly positive approach to life, his ability to focus on the good in everything. She didn't think it was necessarily to do with his developmental delay, more likely it was an inherent part of his personality, and she envied him that ability. Perhaps she should try to be a little more like him. She spent so much of her energy worrying about him, worrying that he might be upset or hurt by people's attitude towards him and trying to protect him from that, when in fact Nicky was quite capable of fending for himself.

She nodded her head. She had helped him to become that person, had supported him to find his independence. Now she needed to step back and stop worrying about him so much. Yes, she would continue to be there for him, if he needed it, but as today had shown her, Nicky would equally always be there for her when she needed him.

Putting down her brush and twisting her hair up into

a high ponytail, her thoughts turned to Kyle, causing a slight flutter in the pit of her stomach as she wondered if he would speak to her or avoid her. That was assuming he would be up there with the others, of course. He, too, might be choosing to keep his own company. In the mirror, her eyes shone with unshed tears. Perhaps if he saw how upset she was, he might change his mind?

She frowned at her image, shaking her head sharply. No. Tempting as that thought was, she would not walk around with the pathetic air of a wounded swan. It was time to act with dignity, to accept that he just did not want her enough.

She would not let him know how much his rejection hurt. There was one day of her holiday left; just one more day and night to get through before going home. Her chin lifted. And when she got home, she was going to make some changes.

****

Kyle looked up when Natasha walked into the room, his heart giving two solid thumps in his chest as he caught his breath. She looked stunning in an emerald-green dress, her bare shoulders glowing with a golden tan and, when she sat down next to Lucy, her eyes met his and she smiled. He could only stare at her, marvelling at the way the colour of her dress made her eyes appear huge. His heart ached with longing, but he managed to return her bright smile before she glanced away again and immediately started up a conversation with Lucy.

Was she really as cool, calm and collected as she appeared? She had been so upset earlier; they both had. And he found it difficult to believe she was as relaxed as she appeared.

That smile. That damned smile he had seen a few

times over the last couple of weeks, usually when he knew she was upset or angry with him. He continued to stare at her, looking for any sign that she was not as happy as she appeared, and suddenly wondered at himself.

Why was he concerned that she might actually be as happy and relaxed as she appeared? Surely that would be a good thing, wouldn't it? Was he really so pathetic as to need her to be feeling the same pain as he was? What kind of man did that make him? He had made a choice and he had to live with it. If he was any sort of a decent man, he would be sitting here hoping that her feelings did not run as deep as his.

As he watched, he saw her take a long breath, lifting her chin a little higher, and the relief that flooded through him was immediate; she was hurting as much as he was. She was a fine actress.

Sick to the stomach, he stood and walked over to the bar to pour two glasses of whisky, glancing over at the cosy scene in the salon as he did so.

Nicky was once again trying to teach Nader and Mahmoud how to play Ludo, and Natasha and Lucy were watching with amusement. A lump formed at the back of his throat as he realised how much he was going to miss being a part of this, being part of a family again. Downing his whisky, he topped it up with a steady hand before taking both glasses and walking back to the seating area. He held out the second glass to Natasha. She looked up in surprise, her eyes meeting his for a long moment, perhaps in shared remembrance of the night he had taught her about the different types of whisky. She hesitated only briefly before taking the glass from him with a smile and a murmur of thanks.

"Right, now that we're all here." Nicky grinned and reached beneath the coffee table to pull out a travel board game. "We're going to play Cluedo."

Kyle couldn't help but smile as Nader and Mahmoud both looked at each other in bemusement while Nicky enthusiastically began explaining the rules to them. Once again, his gaze automatically sought Natasha's, but she was busy setting up the game and handing out pencils to everyone, her own gaze fixed on Nicky and shining with affection. Kyle straightened his shoulders, determined to follow her example and stop feeling sorry for himself. He edged his chair closer to the coffee table.

"Right, bags I'm Miss Scarlet."

Nicky stopped in mid-sentence, his jaw dropping as he looked at Kyle. "Miss Scarlet? But, she's a girl."

"I know. But I've always wondered what it would be like to have long, blonde hair." He pretended to sweep long hair from his shoulders. "I think it would suit me, don't you?"

****

Natasha stifled a yawn as the Jeep pulled into the car park at the Valley of the Kings site just after 8am the next morning. Kyle had warned them that, unlike the majority of places they had visited so far, it was likely that this most famous of ancient Egyptian sites would be busy with tourists, so they had decided to arrive early to avoid both the rush and the worst heat of the day. He had also instructed them to ensure they were well covered with sunscreen and hats, explaining that the Valley of the Kings was notorious for leaving unsuspecting and unprepared tourists with sunburn and sunstroke by virtue of the sheer rock faces of the valley drawing down the

171

searing heat.

Kyle shrugged a rucksack over his shoulder, and started walking up the tarmac path towards the tourist bazaar lining each side of the road towards the site entrance. When Nicky hurried to join him, Natasha turned back to assist Lucy from the car, reluctantly dragging her gaze from Kyle's broad shoulders as he strode away. Last night had been exhausting, her face had ached from the constant effort to smile and act as if nothing was wrong. She had been aware of Kyle's almost constant gaze, but on the odd occasion she had dared to glance at him, had been surprised to find that he wasn't looking at her at all. Still, the feeling had persisted, and she was relieved when Lucy had declared she was going to bed. Natasha had quickly followed and, surprisingly, had fallen asleep the instant her head touched the pillow.

"Is everything all right, Natasha dear?"

She looked at Lucy in surprise as the older woman slammed the door shut, and they made their way towards the site entrance. "Yes, everything's fine. Why do you ask?"

"Well, I can't help noticing that you and Kyle are…well, not exactly avoiding each other, but…not as close as you were."

"Oh no, we're fine." She smiled easily at her aunt. "We had a bit of fun, but you know, it's my last day today and there's no point pretending it was ever going to be anything more than a bit of a holiday romance. You said so yourself."

"Oh." Lucy looked a bit surprised. "Well, you're right, of course, but I thought…are you sure you're all right with that?"

"Of course, I'm sure," she laughed, linking her arm

through Lucy's. "Come on, we'd better catch the boys up or we'll lose them."

They managed to pass through the gauntlet of bazaar sellers with relative ease — Natasha wondered if Kyle had warned them to leave the women alone — before catching up with them as they reached the visitor centre. There were already a few tourists around and, talking to the visitor centre staff, it appeared as if Kyle had been right to advise them to visit early, with the site still attracting many tourists each day.

Although still early, the heat was noticeable when they left the air-conditioned visitor centre and made their way along the path winding through the sheer valley hills and cliffs towards the tombs. They fell into their usual grouping with Kyle and Natasha in front, followed by Nicky and Lucy taking a more leisurely pace behind them. Although it felt natural and comfortable, Natasha couldn't help but wish he would catch hold of her hand as he had done so many times before. But he didn't. He walked along beside her, talking softly as he explained about the history of the site and the pharaohs who had been buried with such ceremony in these beautiful tombs.

A little while later, having visited several of the tombs along the main track, Kyle led them back to the car park and, from there, down a narrow dirt track that wound for almost two kilometres through the sheer rock face of the valley. The sun was steadily rising higher in the sky, and Natasha was grateful for her hat and sunglasses.

They were the only tourists walking this narrow path through the cliffs and, when they reached the tomb of Ay, they paused outside for a moment. The air was still and silent, the atmosphere electrifying, and it was easy to understand why this particular place had been chosen as the final resting place of a king.

"This was originally going to be Tutankhamen's tomb," Kyle explained, reaching into his rucksack, and pulling out a bottle of water for everyone. "But, as we know, Tut died unexpectedly and was buried in a tomb not originally designed for him. I know you're interested in Akhenaten and that era, so I thought you'd find this tomb interesting."

Natasha looked at him in surprise, smiling at his thoughtfulness. "I didn't know that. Thank you."

The tomb was bare except for the burial chamber, where there were beautiful scenes depicting Ay fishing in the marshes and hunting for hippopotamus, and one wall with twelve baboons representing the twelve hours of the night. Nicky, in particular, was taken with this painting, and immediately set about recreating it in his sketchbook.

The solemn atmosphere of the tomb seemed to have a sobering effect, and it was a rather subdued group that made their way back to the car park, until Kyle turned to them with a smile.

"So, who's up for a bit of an adventure? We've two options for getting to Hatshepsut's Temple. We can either drive around to the other side of these cliffs, or we can hike across them. There's a path that takes you right across the cliffs, with stunning views from the top."

Lucy waved her hand at him immediately. "Pfssh! You can count me out. My trekking days are over. I'll drive around in the Jeep with Mac."

Kyle turned to Nicky and Natasha. "What about you two? Are you up for it? It's a fair climb, but the view is worth it."

"I'm up for it." Nicky was dancing from one foot to the other, a sure sign he was excited, and Natasha shook her head at him in amusement before turning to Kyle.

"Every time you've told me it would be worth it, you've been right." She lifted her chin and met his gaze. "I'm in."

He held her gaze for a moment before nodding and hitching the rucksack more comfortably on his shoulder. He turned back to Lucy.

"You're sure you don't want to come with us?"

Her response was to raise her eyebrows and pull open the door of the Jeep, and he grinned. "Right then. We'll see you there in about an hour."

****

The rocky path led up from the tomb of Seti I, rising steeply at first, and making Natasha question the wisdom of agreeing to this hike when she began puffing slightly in the oppressively hot sun, falling a little way behind the others. Fortunately, the path gradually levelled out and began to ascend at a gentler incline, and she was able to catch her breath. They saw only one other person on the path — a middle-aged man in shorts and a loose-fitting shirt. Natasha saw Kyle talking to him briefly, but whatever it was Kyle said, the man simply waved a hand and shook his head. With a keen, assessing glance Kyle shrugged and strode on ahead. As she drew alongside the man, he lifted a red, sweaty face to hers and grinned, offering a cheerful hello, which she returned before carrying on up the hill.

The sun continued to beat down mercilessly, and she stopped at regular intervals to take sips of water, glancing at Nicky with amazement at his ability to continue talking, despite his own laboured breathing.

"Nicky, you know, you might find it easier going if you stop talking for a bit." She took a long drink from her water bottle and wiped her mouth with the back of her hand, squinting at her brother in the sun. "You never stop talking."

He took a drink from his own bottle and grinned up at her. "I know. But I've got a lot to say."

"You two okay?" Kyle had stopped a little further up the path.

"Yes, we're coming." She took a deep breath, breathing in the hot, dry air, aware of the sweat trickling along her spine. Heaven only knew what she must look like.

Twenty minutes later they reached the top of the cliffs and, for a moment, she could only sink into a crouch and catch her breath. While the path had not been particularly steep or difficult to negotiate, the heat, the persistent incline, and the arid air, aggravated by the rocky dust kicked up by their boots, had made it an exhausting climb.

"Hey, you okay?" The touch of Kyle's hand on her shoulder sent a thrill of unexpected desire shooting through her, and she stood up quickly with a smile. "I'm fine, just catching my breath…Oh!"

It was the first time she had taken in the view, having been concentrating on putting one foot in front of the other for the majority of their hike up the cliff. The view was simply stunning, with the Nile river lazily snaking across the valley floor, and the ruins of Karnak and Luxor sprawling across the far bank. Taking a step towards the cliff edge, and careful to stay back from the vertigo-inducing drop to the valley floor, she could see the natural amphitheatre created by the crescent shape of the cliffs, within which stood the Temples of Mentuhotep and Hatshepsut.

The beauty of this ancient country was overwhelming, and emotion swelled within her, forming a lump at the back of her throat. Tomorrow she would be leaving all this behind, and returning to the lush green fields of England and a far different kind of history and beauty; albeit one that she loved. But oh, how she would miss this.

She turned to Kyle, tears shimmering in her eyes. "It's so beautiful. I don't want to leave." She gave a tremulous smile before turning back once more to drink in the view.

"I know." He stepped up to the edge beside her, shoving his hands in his pockets. "It had the same effect on me. It was this view that convinced me to stay when I first came to Egypt ten years ago. That's why I never went home."

She turned to him in surprise. "You never went home?"

He shrugged, his gaze far away. "It wasn't much of a home, really. I didn't have any emotional ties to England, no family, no-one special. I was only renting, so there was nothing to stop me."

"Don't you miss England?"

"Sure, I miss it sometimes, and I occasionally fly back to catch up with old friends, but there's nothing there to pull me back."

She blinked and looked away, wincing at the pain those words caused. *Nothing there to pull him back. Not even her.*

"Natasha…"

She shook her head quickly. "And of course, you met Carrie here?"

"Yes, we met on a dig out here. She was an archaeologist, too, so it worked."

Natasha nodded her understanding. She got it. He was trying to give her all the reasons why it wouldn't work for them, curse or not. She took out her phone and started taking photographs, concentrating on ignoring the man standing beside her.

"Hey, give me your phone and I'll take a photo of you two."

Before she could refuse, Nicky snatched the phone from her hands, stepping backwards to line them up in the viewfinder. "Come on, stand a bit closer so I can get you both in."

Kyle's hand slid across her back and around her waist to pull her close against his side and, after a brief hesitation, she wrapped her arms around him to rest her head against his shoulder. If this was her last chance to feel this closeness between them, then she was going to take it.

"Excellent, that's a great photo."

She barely heard her brother as she looked up into Kyle's eyes, his arm still holding her close. She saw his eyes drop lower to fasten on her mouth, and she licked her lips, feeling a sense of satisfaction when his pupils dilated, and his hand tightened on her waist.

"Kyle! Quick!"

Natasha rocked a little at the speed with which he moved away from her in response to Nicky's somewhat panicked cry. He hurried over to where Nicky was clutching the arm of the same man they had passed earlier on the path, and who appeared to be slightly unsteady on his feet. Quickly assessing the situation, Kyle helped the man over to sit on a rocky ledge set a little way off the path, although there was very little shade available at this height on the cliffs. She automatically pulled out her bottle of water and offered it to Kyle, who was crouching in front of the weary tourist.

"Do you have any water?" He asked the man, his lips tightening when he shook his head.

"No, I left it in my bag on the coach."

"Okay, here, drink this." He took the bottle from Natasha with a distracted smile. "What's your name?"

"John." He drank thirstily from the bottle, draining it and sighing in relief as he looked across at Natasha gratefully. "Thanks, I needed that."

"You know it's extremely dangerous to attempt this sort of a climb without carrying any water or sunscreen," said Kyle shortly, reaching into his rucksack. "You've got the beginnings of heatstroke."

"I do feel a bit dizzy, I have to admit, but I thought it was just the climb." John had the grace to look a little sheepish.

"Well, it's not." Kyle looked around for Nicky. "Nicky, can you stand here to the side to try and give John a bit of shade? That's it, great, thanks."

He twisted off the cap of another bottle and poured it slowly over the back of John's neck and shoulders, before taking off his own hat and using it to fan across the man's skin where it was moist from the water. Natasha fished out yet another bottle of water and began to do the same on John's arms and legs, earning herself a smile of approval from Kyle.

After fifteen minutes of fanning and resting, John

declared that he felt well enough to make the rest of the trek down the valley to where his wife would be waiting for him. Gathering their things together, Kyle insisted on accompanying John down safely.

They made their way down the path as it descended in a wide arc around the crescent-shaped cliffs, finally arriving at the ticket office for Hatshepsut's temple. As they approached, they saw Lucy talking to a slim, petite woman wearing white linen trousers and a matching top.

"Oh, John, you were ages, where have you been? You said you were only going to be an hour." She hurried across to her husband. "I was so worried."

"Nonsense. I told you there was nothing to worry about." He laughed off his wife's concern with a shrug and a meaningful glance towards Kyle. "I got chatting to these lovely people up at the top, that's all, and lost track of time."

"Oh, well, I wish I'd known." His wife sighed in irritation and relief. "I was talking to Lucy here, who kept telling me not to worry but you know how I get."

"I do, my darling." John's voice softened as he put his arm around his wife and dropped a gentle kiss on the top of her head. "I do know. And I wish you wouldn't, Sylvia."

He hugged his wife close for a moment before releasing her, and turning back to Kyle, taking his hand and shaking it heartily. "It was good to meet you, Kyle. Good to meet you all." His glance took them all in gratefully, and he leaned forward to whisper a word of thanks out of earshot of his wife, before turning around swiftly and catching hold of Sylvia's hand as they walked across to the ticket office.

"Heavens. She was such a worry wort." Lucy shook

her head in wonder as she watched the couple go.

"With some good reason, it turns out." Kyle said quietly. "He went up there without any water or sunscreen. Luckily, Nicky here saw him looking a bit dizzy and we got him sorted out. I would rather he went back to his coach and rested instead of walking around in the sun."

"I think he's trying to stop his wife from worrying," said Natasha thoughtfully. "She seems a little on edge."

Kyle grunted noncommittally and Natasha smiled. "It was lucky you had so much water in that rucksack of yours. You seem to have a never-ending supply."

"It's a lot lighter now, I can tell you." He smiled begrudgingly. "I wanted to make sure I had enough for everyone here, and anyone else who might be hiking across that valley – I've seen plenty of 'Johns' in my time."

"Yes, you're our hero, Kyle," Lucy said dryly, but softened her sarcasm with a smile. "Come on, look sharp. Let's look around Hatshepsut's Temple and then get back to the boat for lunch, before we all get heatstroke."

****

A few hours later, Natasha stepped from the shower and, wrapping herself in a clean dry towel, padded into the bedroom. It had been another exhausting but wonderful day of sightseeing. Hatshepsut's Temple had been breathtaking, with its stunning double ramp and colonnaded walls cut directly out of the rock face. This had been followed by a leisurely lunch in the blissfully air-conditioned confines of the boat, before making their way across to the other side of the bank to visit Karnak and Luxor.

The scale of the temples was beyond anything she

had yet seen in Egypt and, although her study of the country meant she had a good awareness of the history for these two sites, nothing could have prepared her for the sheer size of the sanctuaries, pylons, and obelisks. Sphinx-lined avenues led to a complex series of courts and rooms, as Kyle took them ever deeper into one temple after another. Easily recognisable from the world of film and television was the Great Hypostyle Hall — a stone forest of columns originally intended to represent a papyrus swamp, but now a forest of silent, stone sentinels of awe-inspiring stature.

Natasha sat down on the small sofa beside her cabin window, once more fishing out her phone to scroll through the photographs she had taken that day. Her heart skipped a beat when the photograph of herself and Kyle, arms wrapped around each other, flicked into view. She had forgotten Nicky had taken that photograph, and she held it up closer, zooming in until Kyle's face filled the whole screen. His blue eyes were looking directly into the viewfinder, and his tanned face was dusty and relaxed as he smiled.

The vision blurred as hot tears filled her eyes, and she threw the phone on the bed in despair, narrowly missing the open suitcase — a further visual reminder of the end of this adventure, as if she needed it.

For a few seconds she allowed herself to cry, slumping back against the wall, but those few seconds were all she would allow herself. Dashing a hand across her eyes, she quickly got dressed and began the depressing task of packing her bag for home.

****

Another early start saw them arriving at Luxor International Airport in good time for the 6.30am flight.

Kyle had slept badly, despite everyone retiring early in readiness for the next morning, and he rubbed his forehead absently, recognising the beginnings of a headache. Having checked in three sets of luggage for the hold, he accompanied them as far as he could to the security check-in, where Lucy turned to him and gave him a brisk hug.

"Thank you so much for a wonderful two weeks," she sniffed delicately. "You take care of yourself bringing that boat back to Cairo, and don't forget to call in and see me when you arrive."

"I will, I promise." Next, he turned to Nicky, who was twirling his hat over and over in his hands. "Right then, Nicky, you look after yourself, and have a safe journey home."

Nicky nodded, his eyes downcast, shuffling from one foot to another. "Okay. When are you going to come and see us?"

Kyle's heart sank and he flicked a glance towards Natasha, expecting an 'I told you so' expression on her face, but she only smiled at him in sympathy before stepping forward.

"Come on, Nicky, you know it's not as simple as that. Egypt is a long way from England, and Kyle has to work. He can't be jumping on an aeroplane to see us every five minutes."

"It's not that far," said Nicky, obstinately. "We're going to be back home for tea today, so it doesn't take that long. Kyle could come to see us on a weekend."

"Nicky…"

"Hey." Kyle touched the younger man's shoulder. "Give me your phone."

Nicky frowned in surprise, but pulled the phone out

of his pocket and handed it to him. He swiped through a few menus before tapping the keys quickly, and then passing it back to Nicky.

"There. You've got my number so you can text me whenever you want." He smiled when Nicky's face immediately lit up. "You can ring me if you want, but it's probably better if you text, because I'm often somewhere without a signal. And don't worry if I don't text you back straight away, okay? It won't be because I'm ignoring you, or don't want to speak to you. I will text you back, I promise."

Nicky was dancing on his toes, hugging the phone to his chest in excitement, thrilled to know he could contact Kyle whenever he wanted.

"But don't be constantly texting him, Nicky," Natasha warned. "Just every now and then, okay? You can't bombard Kyle with texts every minute of the day."

"I know, I know."

Nicky threw his arms around Kyle, who after a moment of stunned surprise, hugged him close, realising how much he was going to miss the young man and his boundless energy.

"You take care of your sister for me, okay?" Kyle whispered in his ear.

"I will. I promise." Nicky grinned before dancing away to show Lucy his phone.

Kyle took a deep breath. This was the moment he had been dreading. He looked at Natasha as she turned from her brother with a smile.

"I guess this is it then?"

He nodded, hooking his thumbs into his jeans pocket as he stared at her, trying to commit her face to memory. She looked as calm and serene as ever, and he wondered if this was another act, and if her stomach was churning as much as his. She stepped closer and caught his hands in hers, smiling up at him.

"I will never, ever forget this holiday, Kyle," she said, squeezing his hands tightly. "And I can't thank you enough for everything you've done, for making it such a wonderful adventure."

She was breaking his heart, and he shook his head. "Natasha—"

"Look after yourself." She looked up at him, and her eyes were bright and clear. "You deserve to be happy. Don't ever forget it. And I hope one day you find someone worth taking a risk for."

Her words stunned him, and he simply stared at her in silence. She returned his gaze steadily for a second before slipping her arms around his neck, at which point he crushed her to him, dropping his head into the curve of her neck and breathing in the familiar perfume.

"Goodbye, Kyle Richardson," she whispered in his ear. Then she pulled away from him, pushing against his shoulders with her hands when he tightened his arms, unwilling to let her go. When he reluctantly released her, she turned away quickly to pick up her hand luggage, walking back to where Lucy and Nicky were waiting patiently.

Standing alone, Kyle watched her walk out of his life without a backward glance; he closed his eyes in agony, swaying slightly as he took in the enormity of never seeing her again.

When he opened his eyes, she was gone.

****

Kyle gazed at the wake rippling the calm waters of the Nile as the boat made its way back towards Cairo.

The pounding in his head reminded him, as if he needed it, of the amount of whisky he had consumed the previous night, before Nader had found him in a local bar and dragged him out. Five years ago, that had been a regular occurrence, a fact which Nader had commented on.

"I don't understand," he had said. "You love her. Why did you let her go without telling her?"

"I can't." Kyle had shaken off his friend's arm angrily. "And you bloody well know the reason why."

"Aah." Nader nodded in understanding, folding his arms solemnly across his chest. "The curse."

When Kyle remained silent, Nader had leaned in close, impatience darkening his eyes. "You know, this curse offends me. You tell me it affects anyone you care about, who you are close to. And yet, you do not fear for I, I who think of you as my brother."

"Nader, I…" Kyle reached out, but Nader had backed away in anger.

"No. I do not wish to talk to you, Kyle." He waved his hand in disgust. "There is no curse, my friend. Only an excuse for your own cowardice."

It had been pretty much the same thing Natasha had tried to tell him. Kyle rubbed a hand wearily over his face, dropping his head in his hands.

What if she was right? What if they were both right, and he had just let his one chance of happiness walk right out of his life forever?

She had been gone for less than forty-eight hours, and already he was falling apart.

"Carrie," he whispered. "Carrie, what do I do?"

The boat continued its slow path along the river, birds flew overhead, and the world kept on turning, as it had for millennia. Kyle lifted his head and gave a humourless smile.

What did you expect?

Movement at the periphery of his vision caught his attention as he was about to turn away, and he held his breath when a yellow butterfly fluttered on the breeze a few feet away. As he watched, it continued its flight towards him, before landing gently on his breast pocket. It rested there for a few seconds before taking off and fluttering away.

His heart was thumping painfully in his chest. Carrie had loved butterflies, but he rarely saw them in Egypt.

What did it mean? Was it a sign?

Chapter Thirteen

Natasha pulled the jumper on over her t-shirt. It was freezing outside, and the forecast was for snow. She smiled when she thought of Nicky's insistence that they go out tonight to the Christmas Market; he was so excited. The smile faded when her glance fell on the photograph frame sitting on her bedside table. It was the one of all four of them together, taken in their fancy dress costumes the night of the party. For a moment the ache in her heart, the one that seemed to be there permanently nowadays, became almost unbearable and she stifled a sob, lifting her eyes to the ceiling as she concentrated on breathing.

It had been three months since that photograph was taken. Three months. It seemed so long ago since they were enjoying those lazy days cruising down the Nile. And yet she could instantly recall the taste of his lips on hers, the feel of his taught, muscular body beneath her hands, and she only had to breathe in to recall the spicy tang of his aftershave.

No-one knew the effort it had cost her to walk away from him that day, to pretend she felt nothing. Seeing Kyle struggling with his emotions had almost caused her own fragile composure to slip, particularly when she had seen his reaction to her words. She had chosen them carefully, had practised them in front of the mirror. Her intention had not been to hurt him, but to try and break through the determination to spend his life alone, to let him know that it was okay to take a risk, even if that risk was not for her. She had walked away from him, feeling as if her legs might give way at any moment, but had deliberately not turned back one last time. She knew if she had done so, she might not have had the strength to leave.

Instead, she had continued the rest of their journey on automatic pilot, arriving at Cairo Airport where Lucy had left for her hotel, and she and Nicky had boarded their connecting flight to Manchester. Finally, after a further three hours driving, they had arrived home, tired and hungry, to order a takeaway meal. Nicky settled down in front of the television, ready to catch up on all the programmes he had recorded, while she had fled to the sanctuary of her room. Only then had she allowed the tears to flow, closing the door slowly behind her before collapsing on her bed and crying as if she would never stop.

To her surprise, Nicky had appeared to accept Kyle's absence better than she had anticipated; better than herself, at least. It was all she could to do stop herself from asking if he had heard from Kyle, particularly when she saw him sending and receiving texts. She was desperate to know if he ever asked about her.

But she didn't dare. *What if the answer was no?*

She also held on to the pathetic hope, buried in the back of her mind, that he might ask Nicky for her number so he could contact her, but three months later that hope had all but died. He had not changed his mind, after all; she was not worth taking a risk for.

But she had not been idle in the three months since

the holiday. Despite everything, that wonderfully exciting, exhilarating, painful, but ultimately uplifting holiday to Egypt had forced her to re-evaluate her life. She found the courage to hand in her notice at the school, and was now studying for a degree in history, and volunteering in the local museum on her days off. She had never been so happy or fulfilled in all her working life, and the only thing that marred her happiness was her longing for Kyle. She longed to talk to him, to tell him all about her plans for the future, the future he had given her the confidence to reach for. But it wasn't to be, and it was something she was slowly coming to terms with.

"Come on, Nicky," she called, pulling on the black, faux fur-trimmed hat. "Are you ready?"

He appeared from the living room, waving his hand at her in frustration. "I've been ready for ages. I'm waiting for you. We're going to be late."

Buttoning up her coat, she looked at him with a smile. "Late for what? It's a Christmas Market, you can't be late."

Nicky shrugged, putting on the fedora that had taken over from the baseball cap as his must-wear item. "I just meant I'm hungry."

"And whose fault is that?" She ushered him out of the door. "I asked you if you wanted to eat before we left."

"If we ate before we left, I wouldn't have space for my waffle and hot chocolate with marshmallows."

"Okay, okay." She tucked a thick woollen scarf tight around her neck as the icy cold air sent a shiver running through her.

****

The large market square was filled with row upon

row of small wooden stalls, like tiny log cabins, all brightly lit with fairy lights, and selling an eclectic range of food, drink, trinkets, and decorations. Fairground rides were clustered at one end of the square, and a large open-air ice rink was positioned at the opposite end.

Despite the relatively early hour of the evening, the market was crowded with people. Flakes of snow were beginning to fall, adding to the festive atmosphere and, as they entered the crowd, Natasha felt her spirits lifting, suddenly grateful for Nicky's insistence on coming, despite the chilly forecast.

"Tash! Tash, look." Her brother pointed towards the ice rink, turning to her with shining eyes. "You've got to have a go."

Natasha shook her head. "Gosh, no, I don't think so. I haven't skated for years. I'd probably fall over and make a fool of myself."

"No, you won't. You'll be great. Go on."

"No, not tonight, Nicky."

His face fell. "Oh, but you've got to. You're going to go ice skating, and I'm going to have a waffle with squirty cream and a hot chocolate with marshmallows."

She looked at him with sudden understanding. "Like we used to?" When he nodded his head enthusiastically, she gave a resigned sigh and tucked her arm through his. "All right, come on. Let's see what this ice rink is like."

****

She hadn't been joking when she told Nicky she was worried about falling over. It was over ten years since she had last skated, and now stepped out on to the ice with some trepidation. But the moment her skates touched the ice, she felt at home. Whirling around the ice, with the cold breeze brushing her cheeks, Natasha felt the same sense of freedom she remembered from years previously. Nicky had been right; this was what she needed. Unable to keep the smile from curving her lips, she weaved in and out of the other skaters, gaining in confidence and happiness as she dared to put in a few twists and turns.

Ten minutes later, happy but out of breath, she caught sight of Nicky leaning against the railing, eating a waffle piled high with cream. She skated across to him, drawing to a halt with a flourish at the edge of the rink.

"Wow, I'm so out of breath. It's been a long time since I've done so much exercise."

Instead of answering her, Nicky glanced up at the tall man standing beside him, and Natasha followed his gaze, the smile slipping from her face when she was hit by a thrill of recognition.

Kyle.

For a moment, she could only stare at him in disbelief, wondering if she had finally lost her mind and started to hallucinate.

"Hey." His voice was so soft and familiar that it took just one word to break the frozen spell she was under, and she jumped in surprise. Her skates slipped on the ice at the sudden movement, and she flailed for a moment before grabbing the railing, her cheeks burning with embarrassment.

"Hey, be careful." Laughter bubbled through his voice. "You okay?"

"Kyle." She couldn't take her eyes from his, couldn't believe he was actually here. Oh, but he looked wonderful. In place of the usual battered fedora, he wore a black, close-knit woollen hat and, in deference to the chill evening air, a dark reefer jacket and khaki scarf. Just the sight of him standing there brought a lump to her throat, and she was overwhelmed with longing. She desperately wanted to reach out to him, to confirm he was real, but the memory of his rejection still burned, and she didn't dare.

Why was he here? Could it possibly be for her, or was it to see Nicky? The thoughts whirled around her head in quick succession. *Surely not for her, not after three months.*

"Why are you here?" She hadn't meant it to sound so blunt.

He frowned slightly, acknowledging the edge in her voice. "You forgot a couple of things when you left. I thought I'd return them."

She blinked in surprise and confusion. "You…what did I forget?"

"I'm going to get my hot chocolate," Nicky interrupted, licking his fingers as he shoved the last piece of waffle into his mouth. When neither Kyle nor Natasha responded, he shrugged and left them to it.

Kyle dug his hand into his jacket pocket, pulling out a long, red gauze scarf. "You left it tied to one of the chairs on the sundeck." He gave a crooked smile. "It smelled of you, your perfume, but it's faded now."

He held it out to her, and she automatically took it from him. "You came all the way out here to give me a scarf?"

He shook his head, for the first time looking a little hesitant. "No, you left something else, too."

The crowd continued to jostle around them. Skaters whirled around the ice rink, while some of the more nervous ones, clinging to the railing for dear life, tutted when they were forced to let go and totter around her.

But she was aware of nothing other than the man standing in front of her.

"You left my heart behind."

Natasha drew in a sharp breath, unable to believe what she had heard. *Did he mean...?*

"I didn't leave it behind," she said eventually, her gaze fixed on his. "You wouldn't let it go."

Kyle acknowledged her words with a slight nod, dropping his gaze for the first time. She stared at him, aching for him, a tiny spark of hope flickering in the pit of her stomach, and suddenly she was impatient to get closer, irritated by the railing creating a barrier between them. She pushed away and began to skate across the rink.

"Natasha, wait."

Skating smoothly to the exit, she quickly unlaced and handed across the skates, waiting impatiently for the attendant to give back her boots, before pushing her way through the crowd to where Kyle waited. Relief flooded his face when she appeared in front of him.

"You had me worried for a second." He reached for her hands. "I thought you'd gone."

She closed her eyes briefly, fighting the urge to step into his arms. "Why are you here, Kyle? I don't understand why you're here. Why now?"

She watched him take a deep breath, his fingers tightening momentarily on hers, before he dropped his hands. "I'm here for you. I've been lost without you. Everything you said. You were right."

"Right about what?"

"Everything." He shrugged helplessly. "I love you, Natasha. I've loved you since the moment I met you, I just didn't want to admit it. I was so afraid I'd lose you."

Natasha stared at him, speechless, her knees threatening to give way as joy spread through her. She didn't know what to say, and simply stood looking at him.

"You said you wouldn't follow me back here."

"I know. I was wrong," he said softly. "But you're the one. You're the one worth taking a risk for."

Tears of relief and happiness filled her eyes, but she still wasn't quite ready to believe him. "But why now? What changed?"

He caught hold of her hands. "I did. I changed. I've been such a fool." He squeezed her fingers tightly. "So much so that I almost lost you."

When she remained silent, he pulled her towards him gently. "Tash, please say I'm not too late. I wanted to follow you straight out here, but I had to do it right, to prove to you, after everything I said, that I was wrong."

"I want to believe you, Kyle, I really do, but—"

"It's taken me three months to sort everything out, but I have now," he said quickly. "I didn't want to just turn up here and expect you to…I don't know, expect you to be waiting for me. It's taken me this long to finish up some work in Egypt and sort out a contract to lecture across here for a year. I'm renting a house not far away. Nicky helped me a bit there."

"Nicky? Nicky knows about all this? But he's rubbish at keeping secrets." She gaped at him. "And wait…what did you say? A year? You're moving here?"

He nodded. "I told you there was nothing pulling me back here, and there wasn't. But there is now." He drew her into his arms at last and, when she looked up into his eyes, she recognised the uncertainty, felt it in the slight tremor of his body. "I'm terrified, Tash. What if I was

195

right all along about the curse? What if I was wrong? I'm just bloody terrified full stop. All I know is that I can't bear to be without you."

He paused for breath, his gaze electrifying her into silence. "I know I've hurt you, and I know I've got a lot of work to do to prove that I'm worth taking a risk for. But, will you give me a chance to prove it?"

This was it. This was the moment she had dreamt of. She could see his fear, but she felt none; there was no curse. Just a man who had suffered terrible loss in his life, but who was willing to risk everything for her. She took a deep breath and snuggled closer into his arms. "And just how do you intend to prove it?"

She immediately felt him relax.

"Well, I thought I'd start like this." He dropped his head and kissed her — a gentle, lingering kiss that ended far too soon.

She giggled when he lifted his head. "Hmm, not bad. But I think I'm going to take a lot more persuading than that."

"I was counting on it," he murmured, dipping his head to kiss her again.

"Oh Kyle, I've missed you," she whispered, when they eventually paused to draw breath. "I've missed you so much."

He was pulling her in closer, when a large paper cup overflowing with marshmallows was thrust between them.

"Look how many marshmallows they've put on my hot chocolate." Nicky was dancing on his toes. "And thank goodness you've put a smile back on Tash's face. She's been in a right mood since we got back from Egypt."

"And you, Nicky Morgan," said Natasha, attempting to sound cross. "I've a bone to pick with you. What have I told you about keeping secrets?"

A word about the author...

I love to write heartwarming, contemporary romance and romantic suspense novels, with characters I really want my readers to engage with. I live in the beautiful East Riding of Yorkshire in the UK with my husband, and when not writing, enjoy wandering around antique fairs and old stately homes - always on the lookout for inspiration for my next novel.

I enjoy engaging with both readers and other authors, and am a proud member of the Romantic Novelist Association.

http://elliegrayauthor.wordpress.com